DISCLAIMER
IF ROUGH SEX, AN INTERRACIAL PAIRING (BLACK
WOMAN/WHITE MAN), D/S, AND BDSM ARE OF NO
INTEREST TO YOU, YOU SHOULD BYPASS THIS STORY.
INTENDED FOR A MATURE AND KINKY AUDIENCE.
RECOMMENDED FOR ADULTS 18+

THE SWEETEST TABOO

AN UNCONVENTIONAL ROMANCE

HARPER MILLER

THE SWEETEST TABOO
An Unconventional Romance
Copyright © 2014 by Harper Miller

Cover Art and Promotional Materials for *The Sweetest Taboo* created by Taria A. Reed

Editor:
Daphne W. for My Passion's Pen

Copy Editor:
Alison Velea

Formatting:
Bey Deckard for Bad Doggie Designs

Cover Models:
Tayo Oredein
and James Rizzo

ISBN: 978-0-9975447-0-1

A Note from the Author

While writing these pages, I took a backseat and allowed my characters tell their story. The format in which I wrote this story follows my characters' narratives. My writing style may be off-putting to some. You will notice that the name of my heroine, micah, appears in lowercase letters throughout the tale despite the rules of grammar. This occurs when she refers to herself and when Rick refers to her. micah refers to Rick using capitalized pronouns. You will also notice when referring to Himself, my hero, Rick, uses capitalized pronouns but when speaking of, to, or about micah, He uses lowercase pronouns.

In some D/s circles, this is common when writing text. It is not the standard, and not all people use this method when writing. Some even take umbrage to its usage. I chose this method to denote the Dominant and submissive dynamic in the relationship. This style of writing will not be everyone's cup of tea and I am fully aware of that fact; however, it is authentic to my writing process. I wanted to provide readers of this novel some insight into my methodology. With that said, I hope it does not detract from your reading experience.

Thank you for purchasing my novel.

Happy Reading!

A Little Backstory

Every couple is asked about how they met and fell in love. My wife and I are no different.

I don't mind telling the story, but after repeating it so many times, it can become tedious. We were offered the opportunity to share our story with the masses when My old friend Mistress Carlisle asked to interview micah and Me as part of Her "Lifestyle D/s Couples" segment on the syndicated radio show She hosts. Our interview would also be tied into Her BDSM-themed blog.

I agreed to do the radio interview while micah agreed to do the write-up of our story for the blog.

After writing her side of things, micah asked Me to contribute My point of view, as I remember it, and here you have both.

Of course, My pretty girl never does anything halfway, and a couple of blog posts turned into a novel of sorts, and makes for an entertaining read for seasoned players and newbies alike.

Mistress Carlisle enjoyed it so much that She suggested we publish it, and passed the manuscript off to a friend of Hers who runs an independent publishing company. So here we are.

Ours is an unconventional love story. . . .

Yours in Kink,
Master Rick

Contents

Prologue   pg. 1
The Meet and Greet   pg. 9
Playtime   pg. 72
Aftercare   pg. 154
Epilogue   pg. 176

Prologue

Summer 2012

micah

He used the remote control to turn on the entertainment system. In an instant, Prince's "Insatiable" dripped from the hidden speakers of our bedroom.

my Master had already removed His shoes and socks and was in the process of unbuttoning His shirt. Quickly removing the white dress shirt, He tossed it on top of the dresser before stalking toward me.

His pectoral muscles twitched as He moved and i averted my eyes. my sky-blue nail polish shimmered, then was cloaked in my Master's shadow.

i chanced a glance up and was met with a stern but sparkling stare. i was done.

"On your knees, pretty girl."

Nude as the day i was born, i slowly knelt on the plush, cream-colored carpet. His taut abdominal muscles flexed involuntarily as He towered over me. His muscular frame was imposing. i was thrilled to have Him so close. i hadn't seen my Master in two weeks. Being without His touch for two weeks was torture.

His work had taken Him out of the country for a conference, but i knew once He returned, He would want to reclaim me. After an extended period away, His carnal desires always took center stage. i have to admit i looked forward to those times.

i sat back on my haunches with my eyes downward, per protocol, while i awaited His next command. i leaned into the palm of His slightly calloused hand while He caressed the side of my cheek.

"Has My pretty girl missed her Master?" He asked.

"Yes, Sir."

Although my eyes were downcast, they were fairly level with His open suit pants. i loved when my Master was excited to see me. The outline of His erection in the gray boxer briefs told me just how much He had missed me.

He gripped a handful of my hair and twirled it around His fist. my scalp burned, but it didn't matter. He knew i liked it rough. We had an understanding.

"Look at Me, micah," He commanded.

i glanced upward into His baby blues just before He slid His thick and erect penis over the waistband of His underwear. "I want to fuck your mouth before I bury Myself in that tight little cunt of yours. Do you understand Me?"

"Yes, Sir," i replied, nodding eagerly. He pushed my face toward His erection and my tongue maneuvered over the mushroomed tip of His penis while He nudged His way into my mouth. i reached out to take hold of His length when i was quickly reprimanded.

"No hands. Just your mouth, micah," He growled.

i tried to respond but His dick slamming into my mouth quickly cut off my words.

Dear God, i think i felt my teeth rattle.

i placed my hands on His thighs to hold myself upright while He pounded His length down my throat. i was thankful that i kept up my practice of deep-throating the dildo while He was away. Had i not, i had the feeling i would be in serious trouble right now.

my saliva created a thin film around His dick and my eyes began to water. "That's My pretty girl. Fuck. your mouth does amazing things to Me, micah." He grunted, His hands forcefully gripping the sides of my face. One of His hands moved from my face to grip my hair. my mouth and throat were at His mercy, causing tears to fall.

i gasped for every breath.

Just as quickly as His assault began, it ended.

my Master withdrew His dick from my mouth with a loud pop and stumbled away from me, hunched over and breathing heavily. He rested His hands against His muscular thighs. Through my blurred vision, i could see His dick glistening with my spit.

After my Master got His wits about Him, He spoke. "No more, micah, or I'll cum before it's time. Goddamn, that mouth of yours is something."

We were just getting started, and i was so incredibly hot for Him.

With proper posture, chin up and eyes downcast, i leaned back on my haunches with my hands resting on my thighs. During my training a few years ago, my Master stipulated that some version of my stance was proper protocol for most submissives and slaves, but of course, every Dominant was different in His or Her requirements.

He tucked His dick back into His boxer briefs and walked toward me. He slowly advanced and i could feel His eyes studying me. Pulling a handkerchief from His back pocket, He lightly gripped my chin and wiped my mouth, then He used the handkerchief to wipe away my tears.

"My pretty girl," He whispered softly, caressing my chin.

He knelt, which put me slightly below eye level for Him. i didn't dare look at Him without permission. Instead, i kept my eyes on the carpet. Lately, my Master loved eye contact restriction. While it was a subtle way for Him to assert His power, it drove me mad. i loathed not being able to look at Him; however, it wasn't about my desires. He ran the show.

"Look at Me, sweetheart," He commanded.

Finally, i could look into those baby blues i'd come to love so much.

"I've missed you, micah."

i licked my lips but didn't reply. He had given me permission to look at Him but not to speak. i would never be presumptuous enough to speak without His permission.

"you may speak, micah." As always, He read my mind.

"i've missed You too, Master. This girl always misses You when You're away."

He leaned in. my Master's lips softly brushed against mine, sending a tingling sensation down my spine. The kiss He honored me with wasn't too soft or too rough—it was perfect, like most of His kisses. It was filled with need and contained the perfect mixture of lust and passion. He pulled away from me and rose to His full height before walking over to the bed and fetching His belt.

"your Master is very pleased with your performance thus far, micah. I've had the appetizer, now I want the main course."

Based on the intense look in His eyes, i didn't think we were going to make it to the playroom. my Master looked like a starving Man. i guess in theory that was true: i was His meal, and He was ready to devour me.

my Master pulled me up from the floor by my hair and, with a fistful of my tresses, guided me to the bed. "Climb up," He commanded.

"Face down, ass up, micah. your hands should be outstretched in front of you."

i positioned myself as instructed.

He caressed my round bottom and kneaded my asscheeks as if they were the finest dough known to man.

i had made certain that for His return home, i presented myself in a state that was most enjoyable to Him.

"Look at My pretty girl's pussy. Did you wax for Me, micah?" He asked. If i didn't know better, i'd think my Master was smiling.

i nodded, pressing my face down into the duvet. i felt the residual sting from the slap He delivered to my right asscheek. It hurt so good.

"Speak, micah."

my reply was muffled in the duvet. "Yes, Sir. i waxed just for You. i know it's what You prefer."

"you're like a lollipop. So fucking sweet. you're wet for Me, sweetheart, and I intend to see how many licks it takes to get you to lose control."

Reaching for His belt, my Master leaned across my back, pulling my outstretched arms together as He bound them tightly. i felt the bed shift as He got up, but a moment later He returned to bind my ankles together as well.

The feel against my skin made me think He selected the jute rope to bind my ankles. When i was hogtied and during most of our heavier bondage scenes, jute was preferred; it didn't leave rough indentations on my skin.

Once i was restrained to His satisfaction, He vacated the bed. i heard rustling behind me. Thinking of Him standing naked behind me was thrilling. i was anxious for Him to take what was rightfully His.

He returned to the bed where i was bound for His pleasure. i felt His warm breath against my pussy while He used His thumb to massage my clit.

"My pretty girl and her pretty pussy," He murmured seconds before burrowing His face into my cunt.

my Master's tongue swirled expertly against my clit. He licked and sucked my pearl until i was on the verge of succumbing to the overwhelming pleasure. His tongue stabbed me in the most delightful places in the most delightful way.

He ground His face, rough from travel, into me, alternating between licking, jabbing, and swirling His tongue around my pussy, the scratch of His stubble making me hyperaware of every movement. With His hands cupped around my hips, my Master lifted me to give Him more access. Suckling on my pussy lips, He inhaled deeply and then let out a long, low moan against my sex.

i wanted to scream. i wanted to moan. i wanted to growl. i wanted to shout to the heavens, but i wasn't granted permission to speak. If my erratic breathing were any indication, you would think i was experiencing the onset of an asthma attack. It had been a while since i'd had an attack, but if i didn't control myself, this situation would go from pleasurable to concerning in a moment's notice.

i pushed my backside further onto His face as His tongue continued to impale me, riding my Master's face as if my life depended on it. The sounds of Him feasting on my womanhood echoed throughout the room.

"you want to cry out, don't you, micah?" He asked while swirling His tongue tortuously slow around my clit. i was His violin, and He played me beautifully.

i was unable to do much of anything aside from whimper, which came out sounding like erotic hiccups.

His tongue made swift motions against my clit as He maneuvered my body to insert two fingers into my wet channel. "you want to cum, don't you, pretty girl? The way your pussy is gripping My fingers tells Me that My girl wants to cum . . . badly. you're fucking soaked, micah."

Another soft whine escaped my lips as He ferociously finger-fucked me. Oh God, the wonderful agony.

my orgasm steadily built, pushing me to the brink of tears. i was close, so close, but i was forbidden to come without my Master's explicit permission.

Orgasm denial was something i both loved and loathed. my body was His and would do as He commanded.

In a hurried move, He pulled His fingers from my slick channel and shifted His body to fill the void. He never much cared for allowing me time to accommodate His size in the heat of the moment.

i was immobile as my Master pounded my pussy, using a fistful of my hair for leverage. Sweat coated both our bodies as He fucked me vigorously.

"Fuck, it's been two weeks since I've been inside this pretty pussy. Two very long weeks."

my scalp burned, my knees weakened, and i was on the verge of collapsing. my orgasm was so close. It took everything in me to keep it at bay. While i had a love-hate relationship with most of His punishments, i didn't want to upset Him by coming without Him granting me the honor.

my Master continued to ride my ass . . . *hard.*

He gripped my waist tighter while thrusting into me. God, He was so deep, i hurt, but it felt so damn good.

"I love fucking you, micah. I never get tired of seeing My dick going in and out of your pretty pussy. We make a beautiful sight, pretty girl; the contrast of our skin tones always turns Me on."

i whimpered into the duvet cover and struggled to remain upright.

"Let Me hear you, micah. I want to hear you come for Me, pretty girl. Come for your Master."

His permission was all i needed. With His allowance, i screamed as if i were possessed by the Devil. If the neighbors happened to hear us, they would likely think my Master was committing bloody murder. Murder was happening all right—He was slaying the hell out of my pussy. i don't think i'd ever come so hard in my life.

Before i had the chance to enjoy the mesmerizing post-orgasmic bliss, my Master sped up His pace. His grunts, groans, and expletives let me know that He found pleasure in His release.

After catching His breath, He slowly withdrew from me, making certain to keep my ass high in the air as i felt a trickle of cum slide down my inner thigh.

"I want you to stay in this position, micah, and lift your ass higher. I lost a little bit when I pulled out, but keeping your ass in the air for a spell will help with sperm motility," He commented while tenderly removing the rope and belt from around my limbs.

i formed a small smile. "Sperm motility"? Who says that?

Once finished, He rose from the bed and went into the bathroom. Without making a sound, i remained in the position as instructed for the next fifteen minutes until my Master returned and pulled me down alongside Him.

He kissed my lips and forehead softly as He lowered my body on top of His rigid chest. i could smell and taste myself on His lips.

"you may speak freely."

"That was amazing, Sir," i replied, beaming.

my Master laughed. "I'd say so. Absence makes the heart grow fonder and My dick grow harder. Both are needed for baby-making."

i chuckled at His comment.

He had a way with words. He caressed both my wedding band and engagement ring before linking His fingers with mine.

With my free hand, i fiddled with the thin silver necklace around my neck. my collar.

my heart fluttered.

"I've only been home a few hours, but I think this 'welcome back' sealed the deal. If it hasn't and we have to try this every single night for the rest of the month, I'm all for it. I *will* get you pregnant."

"i have no doubt about that, Sir," i said, giggling.

The Meet and Greet

her Master

It was one hell of a Saturday night. A five-car pileup on the FDR Drive had My ER running at a frenetic pace. After the shit I endured today, I needed to take the edge off.

My nose and throat burned from the carbonation and raw ginger of My hand-mixed ginger ale. I'd been at Spanxxx for about an hour and on My third drink; I'd have a good buzz if the club allowed alcohol, but liquor and play don't mix. That's how it'd been here since they opened their doors thirty years ago. It was the policy at most fetish events, but at private parties, the rules were dependent on the host. C'est la vie.

The few men sitting near Me halted their conversation and not so discreetly turned toward the door. My gaze followed theirs. I scanned the crowd to see what they were focused on when My eyes fixated on her.

she looked stunning standing at the entrance of the club, assisting her female companion with the hem of her skirt. I continued to follow the ladies with My eyes, pausing while they offered their identification to the bouncer.

Men and women gawked at the pair as they moved through the club. I'm pretty sure they all saw what I saw: a submissive looking for a home.

How did I know she was a sub? she didn't make direct eye contact with anyone, she kept her gaze constantly fixed ahead, and she only spoke to her companion. I could be completely wrong in My assumption, but she didn't strike Me as a Domme. I didn't get that vibe based on what I'd witnessed thus far.

I had been in the scene for a while, so I could usually tell. When Your friends consisted of a variety of lifestyle and pro-Dommes, You picked up a thing or two. It might sound pretentious, but it was the truth. In addition, in My profession, I had to be adept at reading people. I considered it a gift and a curse.

Worst-case scenario, I'd find out during the auction if My instincts were on point. I assumed that's why she was here, since tonight's featured event was a sub/slave auction.

I casually took another sip of My drink and wondered if she would prove to be a worthy challenge.

Was she merely a submissive, or was she a slave? I sincerely hoped the former. Not that I found anything wrong with slaves; I just didn't have an interest in dictating someone's life twenty-four seven. In many instances, I would prefer My girl be left up to her own devices.

I would never knock anyone for the dynamic they chose. However, My nature was to lead, not lord over, so My girl would have to have a life and interests of her own. Taking a slave was never what I considered an ideal arrangement. But before I got ahead of Myself planning for the future, I needed to find out on what side of the line My pretty girl stood.

I continued to watch her while I fiddled with the ice in My empty glass. I don't think I could have taken My eyes off her if I wanted to. The fitted pink blazer she wore barely concealed her corset, which pushed her breasts up in a way that made Me shift in My seat. My gaze traveled higher to her unadorned neck. The dim light of the club made her skin glow.

she licked her utterly sinful-looking lips. I licked My lips as well.

her dark hair was pulled away from her face in a tight chignon. Due to the lighting, I couldn't tell if the color was black or dark brown, but from where I was sitting, it seemed to have a wavy texture. her smoky eye makeup gave her an air of mystery and her pouty gloss-covered lips were turned down in a frown.

In that moment, I wanted to see her smile. A face like that should never have a frown upon it.

Shit, she was gorgeous, and not in that ostentatious way that I'd been accustomed to.

she wasn't someone I'd normally appraise, but she captivated Me the moment she stepped through the club doors. I hadn't dated many women of color, and by "dated" I mean courted. I had a few romps in the hay but nothing significant or lasting.

When it came to dating, I hadn't expanded My horizons. My track record consisted mostly of thin brunettes and a few blondes. Occasionally, a redhead would thrill Me, but this woman . . . she was different from the women I usually found attractive. Aside from her physical differences, she possessed a unique style I found charming.

A smiled curved My lips as I continued to observe her—the woman was sexy as hell. I willed the beautiful vision before Me to bend over. And as if she heard My silent request, she tucked her purse under her arm and bent at the waist to adjust her garter belt and sheer black thigh-highs. A pair of ruffled panties that matched the color of her blazer peeked out from underneath the short skirt she wore. My mouth watered as My eyes scanned the entire length of her body all the way down to her stiletto-clad feet.

she was petite with an hourglass figure, and reminded Me of a classic pinup: neither rail thin nor too big. her body was what wet dreams were made of. If I were to take a guess, her height hovered somewhere around five-foot-three.

her angelic face hardened when she was seized by a coughing fit. Apparently, the cigarette smoke of nearby patrons was bothersome. The air-conditioning in Spanxxx was flowing comfortably but the air-filtration system didn't seem to be aiding the cocoa-colored beauty.

she continued to cough while her companion leaned over her and rubbed her back. From My observation, it looked as if her companion was asking if she was okay. Despite her rich skin tone, the coughing fit seemed to redden her face.

The beauty's companion left her alone and made a quick trip to the bar. her companion stood next to Me, squeezing in between a few patrons, and requested a bottle of water. The bartender grabbed a bottle from behind the bar and handed it to the woman. she handed the bartender what looked to be two dollar bills, grabbed the water, and headed back to the gorgeous vision. The beauty accepted the offering and chugged the water.

As I watched her, My dick stirred in My pants. What can I say? I was turned on watching those full lips wrap around the bottle.

Oh, to be that bottle . . .

micah

my week had been hellish with prepping for the new exhibit and all the other things my boss threw my way. i swear Joan Holloway must have believed i had been put on this earth to serve her.

i was no stranger to hard work. my job as an assistant registrar kept me in high-pressure situations, but managing projects, staff, and her craziness had gotten to me. Thank God for kisa and her horny, crunchy, granola-eating self. For months she'd flooded my email with invitation-only fetish events. i guess she considered my dating life to be pathetic and worried that i'd end up as a shut-in with an assortment of vibrators and cats to pass the time.

kisa, that girl . . . i absolutely love her to death, but good grief, her legs spread like butter. Many a Dom has had her Country Crock. Tonight, she was about getting laid, and i was about letting loose with a new friend and a little play.

Spanxxx was hosting a sub/slave auction, and kisa had guilted me into signing up after she learned i had been spending most nights alone drinking wine like it was going out of style. Private collectors can be some of the most unbearable prima donnas. Coordinating loans from overseas institutions, working for a curator who had a habit of throwing everything but the kitchen sink my way, and handling an overstressed staff had me not only drinking more than usual, but i also used my rescue inhaler twice this week. In the past, even in the midst of high-stress situations, i hardly touched the thing. miss holistic, yoga guru, said i needed to make room for meditation in my life, that maybe it'd help get my asthma under control. But before kisa lead me on a path to Zen, i figured i should make an appointment with my doctor for a checkup.

Monday. Real-life concerns could wait until Monday.

It was Saturday night, and fun was on the agenda. The controlled environment of the club ensured that myself and other subs and slaves were treated with respect and care. If a Dom or Domme, whatever the case may be, was interested, They'd bid to have us for the duration of the event. There would be time to mingle beforehand, and then after the winning bid, we'd go into one of the playrooms. . . .

i'd been around the scene since my early twenties, so now at thirty, i'd pretty much seen and had it all. A great deal of men call themselves Dominants but believe that D/s is *only* limited to the bedroom. In my opinion, a little bit of rough sex or some sort of degradation does not make one Dominant. Too many equate being domineering with being Dominant. The two aren't synonymous. Those "bedroom Doms" can take a hike. i'm not a slut, whore, tramp, bitch, cum dumpster, or any of those other slurs these "bedroom Dominants" hurl at submissive women in a poor attempt to assert power.

There's only so many frogs a girl can kiss, so tonight was all about blowing off steam. i went to Spanxxx with zero expectations. Sure, my long-term goal was to find the right Dom, but i'd rather wait for something real. i'm no doormat and have few self-esteem issues; if you feel the need to try and belittle me to get your rocks off, i am not the one for you.

i looked around the club, trying to make mental note of who might be worth a few minutes of my time; i don't accept mediocrity when it comes to my Men, and wasted time is my only regret in life. i'm also a workhorse type and expect the same in a Dom, but i've run into far too many damaged and domineering jerks instead of ambitious, refined Gentlemen.

i'll readily admit that i am a submissive to anyone who dares to ask, but being submissive doesn't equate to being weak. i'm not some feeble woman who gets off on being demeaned. For me, being submissive meant taking care of my Man's needs in every capacity. It meant bending to His will, and His will only. He would lead and i would follow. i would be perfectly content in my role when it came to pleasing Him, and the Man who captured my heart would be an Alpha down to His core. i would be His servant, His lover, His friend, His everything. He would be my Guide, my Protector, my Confidant, my Love. He would not demand my respect, He would earn it. He would love me for my mind. He would see beauty in both my strengths and weaknesses, and encourage me to be the best version of myself. So you see, this lifestyle went well beyond spankings and tying me to a headboard.

After tucking my ID back into my clutch and adjusting my garters, my lungs were seized by the smoke that hung in the air. The club didn't allow alcohol, but smoking was A-OK. i would have made some smartass comment to kisa if my lungs were working.

A new law had recently been passed that banned smoking in bars and clubs, but it wouldn't go into effect for another month. Until then, i would suffer. After i experienced a coughing fit that damn near brought me to my knees, kisa handed me bottle of water.

i drank quickly, hoping it would help. my coughing stopped long enough for me get my inhaler out of my clutch. Two quick puffs usually helped alleviate the constriction in my chest. i felt a bit overheated so i removed my blazer and tucked it under my arm along with my clutch.

kisa rubbed circles over my bare shoulders. her hand was still cool from the water bottle and was a welcome relief from the steroid hotly racing through my system. "you gonna be okay?"

i nodded and rasped out, "i'm fine. Go have fun. i'm probably gonna go sit at the bar."

she wrapped her arm around my shoulders, giving me a squeeze before whispering in my ear, "i love you. i'll be just over there." she pointed to the plush sofas where a group had congregated.

"All right. Go get 'em."

kisa was gone before i could utter another word.

i took a few moments to get my bearings before i decided it was time for me to scope out the scene as well. As i made my way through the crowd, i felt a clammy hand grip my elbow. The guy who stopped me had a cigarette dangling from the corner of his lips. i immediately removed his hand before turning my nose up and continuing on my path toward the bar.

i was already trying desperately to get my breathing back on track. The last thing i wanted was to start a discussion with a human chimney. In another attempt to initiate conversation, a handsome, clean-cut guy asked if he could buy me a drink. i told him maybe later, before exchanging quick pleasantries. i figured if he was truly interested in getting to know me, he'd put in a bid when the auction started. i hoped the human chimney got the hint—smoking was one of those things that immediately turned me off.

Most people chose to congregate near the bar to get conversation going or to pull up a stool and take in their surroundings. i was hoping for some decent conversation before the auction began. Wouldn't you know, just before i reached the bar, some tool was bold enough to grab my ass? i froze for a moment in disbelief that someone would be so blatantly disrespectful. i whirled around to face my assailant before stepping on his toe with the heel of my stiletto. The man winced as my heel dug into the leather of his shoe. *So you want to palm my ass? That'll teach you to be touchy-feely.* i apologized to the stranger with a sly smirk before walking away. What an asshole. No wonder i don't take these guys seriously. Who violates a woman's personal space like that? It's the antithesis of the behavior a Dom should display.

Where the hell did kisa disappear to?

she moved through the crowd with an air of grace, pausing briefly to speak with men who were momentarily successful in gaining her attention; however, she seemed disinterested in what most of them had to say.

One guy learned the hard way to look but don't touch. He forcefully grabbed her ass, and the little vixen ground her heel into his foot, causing him to flinch in pain.

What a good girl. No man has the right to touch you without your permission. she was feisty—I liked that.

I was ready to pounce in case he decided to retaliate.

As she moved closer to the bar, and by default Me, her balance wavered. she slowed her approach and began coughing again. her coughs turned to wheezing and gasps before she could take another step.

I stood. When her eyes met Mine, I saw panic in her features.

I closed the distance between us and offered My assistance. "Hey, are you okay?"

she didn't respond, but instead began rummaging through her purse.

Of course, I immediately realized she was likely looking for her inhaler.

"Whatever you do, sweetheart, don't panic. Here, let Me help," I said, taking her purse. I was in a better position to find the goddamn thing. "I saw you with an asthma pump a bit ago. Are you a chronic asthmatic?" I asked, locating the pump.

I handed her the inhaler and she took a few quick puffs and as deep a breath as she could before grounding out the words "Can't breathe." her eyes glazed and her legs started to give. I dropped the purse and quickly grabbed her just before she collapsed.

Oh shit. This was *not* happening.

No. No. No.

Fuck.

my legs buckled and my blazer fell from my grasp. Before my body met the floor, a pair of muscled arms grabbed hold of me. The voice attached to the arms shouted at the bartender, "Call 911. We've got an emergency here!"

Nearby patrons hurled questions our way. "Is she dying?" "Does she need CPR?" "What's wrong with her?"

The Stranger attached to the pair of strong arms ignored all their questions and gently lowered me to the floor as a small crowd gathered. He held my head in His lap as tears rolled down my cheeks.

i continued to wheeze, struggling for every little bit of air.

i was going to die on the floor of a fetish club, but all i kept thinking was, *Where the hell is kisa?*

"Shh. Relax, sweetheart," He murmured as He softly stroked my hair. "Relax."

He tried His best to soothe me by speaking calmly. "From what I gather, you're experiencing an asthma attack. Panicking will only exacerbate your symptoms, and that could be fatal."

i was so damn scared. my heart felt as if it were going to pop out of my chest. He held His fingers against my neck. i assumed He was monitoring my heart rate.

"I need you to relax and try your best to breathe through your mouth. Slow and steady. Short breaths."

i concentrated on His voice and stared at His lips to keep me calm. It was the only thing i had at the moment. my mind raced with a thousand different thoughts: *Where the hell is kisa? Why does this Stranger smell so damn good? Why am i laying on this nasty-ass floor? Why does He have such nice lips?*

He was talking, and i had tuned out most of what He was saying but i continued to watch His lips move.

Despite my mind running a mile a minute, i followed His instructions and took short breaths. Breathing wasn't as difficult but it was still an effort. What i was experiencing was easily the scariest moment of my life. my chest ached and my throat felt arid and tight.

If i am going to die tonight, at least i'll have a handsome face as a send-off.

Did i really just think that? Clearly, the panic hadn't lessened, since i was delirious. Thirty was too young to die; i had so much more life to live. i wanted to visit the pyramids in Egypt, i wanted to learn to swim, i wanted to have an M/M/f threesome, i wanted to run the San Francisco marathon, i wanted to try electro torture, i wanted to pierce my nipples, i wanted to get married, i wanted babies, i wanted to be a soccer mom, i wanted so much. . . .

If it was my time to go, i didn't want to be alone. The Stranger was comforting, but i didn't know Him. *Shit, where the hell is kisa?*

As if on cue, kisa screamed at the patrons to let her through. "Holy shit, micah! Oh my God. Oh my God. Oh my God." she was a frantic and hysterical mess.

Most people still stood around gawking as everything unfolded. i didn't like the unwanted attention but there wasn't much i could do about it.

The handsome Stranger continued stroking my hair while frowning at kisa. He addressed her through clenched teeth. "miss, an ambulance has been called and they're on the way. your friend seems to be having an asthma attack, and you panicking while I'm attempting to soothe her is not in her best interest. If you want to help, I'm going to need you to get it together."

Although His tone was clipped and not at all malicious, the piercing look He gave kisa indicated He was serious.

kisa heeded His warning and calmed down, silently sobbing while she held my hand.

"Don't you die on me, micah," she said as tears streamed down her face. "i shouldn't have asked you to come here. This is all my fault."

Oh jeez, i didn't want kisa to feel like she was responsible for what was happening. my asthma attack could have happened anywhere. Since i couldn't respond, i squeezed her hand, hoping she knew i didn't blame her for my predicament.

The ambulance finally arrived and the crowd thinned, allowing the EMTs to pass. The floor seemed to rumble like something mighty was heading straight for me. i caught a glimpse of a yellow-and-black box just before it was placed out of my sight. A man knelt beside my handsome Stranger, but my attention was drawn to the squeak and moan of rubber and metal. i jumped when a gurney fell into my line of sight.

The man to my right took my arm and strapped me to some sort of portable blood-pressure machine. While the device constricted my arm, the EMT asked questions i couldn't physically answer. my handsome Stranger was ready, though. The EMT raised his eyes from my arm and looked at my Hero. His eyes bugged out and his mouth fell open to utter what sounded like "Doctor Thomas." The EMT started to say something else, but my handsome Stranger slowly shook His head. Whatever just happened set the EMT back to his task.

Wait, did he say "Doctor" or was that my imagination? i was a wee bit delirious after all.

"Look, don't ask any questions," the Stranger directed. "Let's just stabilize her and get her to Kincaid Metro's ER. I'll take over until we can get a pulmonologist to assist."

kisa looked over to Him, clearly confused. "You're a Doctor?" she asked.

"I am, and if you're accompanying your friend to the emergency room, we've got to move now."

It wasn't my imagination and i wasn't delirious. He was a Doctor.

Although things could have gone horribly wrong, i felt fortunate that my Hero was a physician. At least if things took a turn for the worse, He had the training to save my life.

i was lifted onto the stretcher and wheeled out of Spanxxx with kisa and the handsome Doctor flanking me. i saw kisa grab my clutch and blazer and was thankful she had a cool enough head to remember my belongings. The contents of my clutch were sprawled out on the floor, but luckily there wasn't much of value other than my ID, twenty dollars, and the keys to my apartment. One paramedic hopped into the driver's seat of the ambulance while the other loaded me into the back of the cab. kisa and the Doctor quickly followed.

Once we were inside the ambulance, the Doctor rifled through compartments. When He found what He was looking for, which turned out to be a small vial filled with a clear liquid, He grabbed a pair of latex gloves and a syringe while kisa and i looked on. He put on the gloves before hiking up my skirt, unclipping my garter belt, and rolling my thigh-high down to my knee. He used an alcohol swab to sterilize a portion of my upper thigh.

i knew what was coming next and i was deathly afraid of needles. Despite being told not to panic, i couldn't help but take frantic breaths.

The Doctor immediately noticed the change in my breathing pattern, and His facial expression registered alarm.

For a big Guy, the handsome Doctor moved pretty fast. He filled the syringe with the clear liquid while the second paramedic grabbed an oxygen mask and fiddled with a few dials.

i tried my best not to get worked up, but i couldn't stop thinking about the needle that was about to pierce my skin. i glanced up and once again focused on the Doctor's lips as He spoke.

"This is epinephrine. It'll pacify your symptoms until we can get you to the hospital. Just continue to breathe through your mouth in short spurts as I instructed," He said while administering the drug into my thigh.

kisa sat quietly watching it all unfold as the paramedic placed the oxygen mask over my face. The small pinch wasn't as bad as i'd thought it would be.

i hadn't realized we'd started moving until the sirens roared to life and the cabin began to sway. The oxygen helped my labored breathing, but danger still lurked, if the way the handsome Doctor watched me was any indication.

Once satisfied that my breathing was stabilizing, the Doctor finally acknowledged the paramedic who recognized Him at Spanxxx. "I'm off duty, Jay. I saw a woman in distress and went to help her. My reason for being at Spanxxx is no one's business."

my gaze volleyed between the two men. This was kinda juicy.

The paramedic fiddled with my oxygen and the Doctor frowned at me. i guess in my nosiness, my breathing picked up.

The Doctor patted my arm and left His hand there. The weight of His paw-size hand pressed onto my flesh, sending a warmth through me.

He turned His attention back to the paramedic—Jay—and spoke in a much softer tone. "What I do in My private life is just that: private. I didn't violate any hospital policies and would appreciate it if you'd respect My privacy by never mentioning to anyone why I'm the admitting physician for this patient on My day off. If asked, I was taking an evening stroll, saw an ambulance outside the club, and offered My assistance. Are we in agreement?"

Jay nodded. "Yes, Doctor Thomas, I understand. I'll relay the information to Bobby when we get to the ER."

"Thank you, Jay," the handsome Doctor replied while glancing down at me, His lips curled upward in a warm smile. If i didn't know better, i'd think He was flirting . . . but there was no way. i was definitely delirious, but it was a nice thought if only for a moment. His smile definitely seemed a little more than friendly.

i watched the two men move silently and in tandem, attending to my needs while we rode to the hospital. Maybe it was anxiety over my present situation. Maybe i was without adequate air too long. Maybe there was something more than just oxygen coming through this mask. Whatever it was had me thoroughly confused by the time we pulled up to the emergency room.

They wheeled me up the access ramp with kisa and the Doctor following closely behind. Although i was pumped full of adrenaline, my eyelids became heavy as i was pushed through the sliding glass doors. i squinted and blinked to shield my eyes from the bright lights—and that was the last thing i remembered.

her Master

Well, so much for initiating conversation and maybe placing a bid on her at the auction. No better way to break the ice than saving a woman's life.

her friend had called her micah. micah. An unusual but beautiful name for a woman and it fit her perfectly. I soon found out her full name: micah marie foster. I chuckled at her initials, MMF. *I'm a dirty, dirty Man.*

It really was amazing the things You find out when You have access to a patient's medical history. I was lucky; micah had been previously treated at Kincaid Metro for a sprained ankle. her gynecologist was also affiliated with the institution. As a physician on micah's medical team, I was privy to a wealth of information— some of it desired and some of it irrelevant.

micah was thirty years old—seven years younger than Me—and unmarried with no children. she had never been pregnant; she had had her appendix removed when she was ten; she had no allergies; she was diagnosed with asthma at seven; her blood type was B positive; she last had a pap smear a month ago and an STD panel run a year ago. her parents were listed as her emergency contact, and she worked as an assistant registrar at the Whitney Museum.

Of course, I was the attending physician for the duration of micah's three-day hospital stay. Well, I worked in conjunction with a pulmonologist to get her asthma under control and handed off care to My most trustworthy residents when I required sleep or had to leave the hospital. I wanted to be sure she was always left in capable hands if I were ever unable to directly oversee her care.

While she was here, I played it cool. Never once did I breach any boundaries of Doctor-patient rapport, but don't think I didn't want to. Professionalism remained at the forefront. I'd wait and feel her out, but I knew one thing for certain: I couldn't let her leave the hospital without speaking with her alone. Once she signed the discharge papers, the Doctor-patient relationship would be severed. I hoped she would be receptive to My offer.

I *needed* her to be receptive to My offer.

I tapped on the frame of the open door. micah was bent slightly at the waist, putting her things into a hospital bag. The sun shone brightly in the room, making whatever she'd put in her curly hair sparkle like tiny crystals.

she looked up from her bag and made eye contact with Me as I walked into her room. God, she was beautiful.

"Afternoon." I shoved My hands down into the pockets of My lab coat before I did something unprofessional. "Are you all ready to go?"

she nodded. "Yes, Doctor Thomas. The nurse brought my discharge papers a few hours ago. i was just heading out, but i'm glad You stopped by. i wanted to thank You for Your help.

"i can't tell You how humbled i am by Your act of kindness. You saved my life, and i will be forever grateful," she said as her eyes darted around the room, looking everywhere but at Me. she shoved a sweater into her bag with less care than she took with her other clothing.

her words were sincere, but for whatever reason, I must have made her nervous, although I wasn't sure why. she gathered the plastic bag and her purse before quickly brushing past Me and exiting the room.

This was not how I envisioned things going. I increased My pace and caught up with micah at the nurse's station. It was all or nothing; I only had a few moments to make an impression.

"ms. foster? micah?" I called out. I composed Myself as I approached her.

she slowed her pace, bid farewell to the nurses, then turned in My direction.

I jumped at the opportunity, unable to wait a moment longer. "ms. foster, I was hoping to speak with you before you left. Once you signed the discharge papers, the Doctor-patient relationship ended. That means I'm no longer your treating physician and you're no longer My patient. With that said, I have a question I'd like to ask. Please hear Me out. Don't take this the wrong way . . ."

her facial expression was unreadable, so I continued.

"I'm not trying to be a creep, but I would regret letting you leave today without at least giving this a fair shot. I sincerely apologize if you feel this is inappropriate or too forward, but ms. foster, I'd love your company for a drink or dinner . . . whichever you'd prefer. Will you allow Me to take you out?"

Waiting for her answer seemed to take an eternity. she didn't look at My face; instead her gaze landed somewhere around the name embroidered on the left breast pocket of My lab coat. her lower lip found its way between her teeth as she stared, apparently deep in thought. In what seemed to be a delayed reaction, she gawked up at My face, clearly surprised by My question.

Was she put off by the entire idea or just caught off guard by My request? Either way, her answer would let Me know which way she was leaning. I just hoped to God she wasn't leaning toward no.

she finally provided Me a small reprieve. "You want to take me out?"

"Yes."

"Like on a date?"

"Yes," I replied again.

"i'm sorry, Doctor Thomas, but i don't date," she said, dismissing Me as she continued to the elevators.

Oh, she was going to make this interesting. her flippant attitude bothered the hell out of Me, but I was going to see this through. I quickly followed in an attempt to catch her before the elevator doors opened and she walked out of My life.

I caught up to her, matching her stride before I spoke in a quiet tone, for her ears only. "I don't date in the traditional sense, either."

she immediately stopped walking and whirled to face Me. There was fire in her eyes; My quick retort clearly riled her up.

Atta girl, maintain eye contact, it shows respect. Now I had her attention.

"i'm not sure i understand what You mean," she replied with tight lips and narrowed eyes.

she actually looked annoyed, which I found endearing. she wanted to make Me work for it? Fine. I could be a good sport. The pursuit was always more fun when it was challenging.

"ms. foster, let's not tiptoe around the obvious—we crossed paths at fetish club. you and I clearly have a lot more in common than we're letting on here, but I understand your reluctance. I'm intrigued and asking to get to know you."

she crossed her arms over her chest as if appraising Me, so I continued. "I'm a Dominant Male seeking a submissive female. The dynamics of the relationship are dependent upon the woman I take as My own and our chemistry. I'm very direct in My needs and desires. I also don't tend to approach My former patients and ask them out on dates. I keep My professional life and personal life separate. This is the first time they've ever overlapped."

micah leaned forward to press the elevator button before briefly turning away from Me.

Goddamnit, would she display some sort of reaction other than indifference? I enjoyed the pursuit but I needed to know if it was worth My time. micah hadn't given Me any indication she was interested. her body language made it seem as if I were a nuisance. Still, I wouldn't drop it until I finished what I had to say.

"D/s isn't an experimental phase for Me. All I'm asking for is an opportunity to get to know you, so we can talk and see if we have similar desires. Will you please grant Me that?"

her shoulders relaxed. Maybe she was warming up to My last statement. I could only assume her indifference was because she thought I was playing games.

her posture straightened, and she had a curious look about her.

It was clear I caught her off guard but, honestly, I wasn't interested in beating around the bush. I wanted her to know I was genuine and not like the dickheads she had likely become accustomed to. I'm sure she didn't know what to think of Me or My offer, but all I needed was for her to say yes, then everything else would work itself out.

she stood before Me, gazing down at her hands while nervously chewing on her lip. she finally spoke, putting Me out of My misery.

"i'm not sure what to make of this, but i'll keep it simple. Can we start with a drink?"

Now we were getting somewhere.

"Yes, we can," I replied, pulling a business card from a pocket of My lab coat, quickly jotting down My cell phone number. "Here's My card, ms. foster."

"Please, call me micah."

"Okay . . . micah." My grin couldn't be stopped, but I didn't want to appear overeager, so I reined it in. "My direct line is on the front. My cell is on the back. I'm covering shifts this weekend, but I'm off Tuesday, Wednesday, and Thursday of next week. I'll be looking forward to your call," I said, handing her My card before taking My leave.

I glanced over My shoulder; she stood there still biting her lip and staring at the card in her hand. That lip-biting thing was fucking hot. her lips already begged to be kissed, but goddamn, I couldn't wait to take a bite. I didn't want to get too excited, but micah was special, I could feel it. My gut had never been wrong about these sorts of things.

micah

i stared at His card. Dr. Richard Thomas, MD, Assistant Professor of Emergency Medicine.

Richard?

Richard seemed way too formal. i had overheard at least two doctors address Him as Rick. In any case, i could see why He preferred to be called Rick. He looked like a Rick. When i thought of the name Rick, i imagined a jock frat boy i might have crossed paths with back in my college days. This Rick wasn't too far from that image. i didn't know about His jock or frat boy status, though i'm sure He possessed some sort of athletic prowess. He looked like He was built for sports.

He was tall, about six-foot-two to my five-foot-three. i was dwarfed next to Him. i had always been attracted to Men who were at least six feet tall. As cliché as it sounds, taller Men represented strength and made me feel safe, secure, and protected.

Every day for three days, i was subjected to the softest blue eyes framed in long, dark lashes. Torture. When He would bend to listen to my lungs, i'm sure i stopped breathing. He'd draw those thick eyebrows together and tighten His chiseled jaw before directing me, in that rumbling bass of His, to breathe deeply.

Now that we had severed our Doctor-patient relationship, He wanted to take me out. i had Him pegged as the type to date models and socialites. i was so far out of my league . . . but He'd said He was a Dom. He had said He wanted me.

Honestly, i found the good Doctor intimidating. From the moment He walked into my hospital room, He had me on edge. i'm not exactly chopped liver, but Doctor Thomas—Rick—was a very attractive Man. You'd have to be blind not to notice, and frankly, i didn't think someone like Him would be interested in me, which was why i stood dumbfounded when He asked me out.

Like i said, i'm not chopped liver, but imagine a chiseled god with mesmerizing eyes asking you out on a date. He was one of those people that kisa and i would classify as really, really, *really* good-looking.

Why did i accept His card? Stepping outside of my comfort zone had never been a problem for me, but this time i wasn't so sure i was doing the right thing.

Later that day, when i told kisa the handsome Doctor who saved my life asked me out, she could only stare at me with her mouth agape. It was cute and funny at first, but around the five-minute mark, i secretly wished a swarm of honeybees would fly into her mouth.

i know it was surprising, but not that damn surprising. i'm not chopped liver, damnit.

Two days had passed and i still hadn't called Him. When we parted, He told me He'd looking forward to my call. i wanted to pick up the phone, but i made an excuse not to each time.

i sat on my loveseat and stared at the business card in my hand. Full disclosure: i was scared shitless.

He wanted to know me.

He wanted to know *me*.

her Master

A little over two fucking weeks and micah still hadn't called. It was maddening. I gave her My business card sixteen days ago and still no call. Sixteen days! Normally, I have no problem being patient, but this shit was ridiculous. I could easily get in touch with her but I left the ball in her court.

she was already skittish about My offer, so I didn't want to spook her by being more forward than I'd already been. I had to move at her pace. micah needed to feel comfortable enough with Me to let her guard down.

I got the feeling she didn't let many people in, so she needed to trust Me before inviting Me into her world. Without trust, there would be no foundation for us to build upon.

The courting process was My favorite part of a relationship. I dug a good pursuit. Women love to be wooed, and I thoroughly enjoyed the Knight in Shining Armor role when she was worth My time. For the right woman, courting would never end.

I hadn't taken on a new submissive in about five years, so I was going to thoroughly enjoy the chase, but micah had to give a little. I could wait her out. she'd call—I could feel it.

My cell phone rang a little after nine just as I was settling down with a beer. It had been a long fucking day; I thought I was done with the hospital for the night. The number was unfamiliar, probably one of My residents with some minor issue that couldn't wait until I was back on duty, so I answered instead of letting it go to voicemail.

"Hello?"

"Uh … uh … um hi, Doctor Thomas, it's micah foster," the soft voice mumbled in My ear.

My dick jerked in My sweatpants. Well I'll be damned. I guess it's true what they say: if You speak it into existence it manifests. Showtime. I'd been waiting for this and it felt good to finally hear her voice.

"Hi micah. Please call Me Rick. It's great to hear from you," I replied. "I was beginning to think you lost My card."

"Um, no i didn't lose Your card. Is this a good time for You, Rick? i can call back tomorrow if that's better."

"No. Right now is perfect. I'm just winding down for the evening. How are you? How are you feeling?"

Shit. Way to go into Doctor mode. I hoped she realized that I was concerned about her overall well-being and didn't take My comment as her treating physician following up. I didn't want that reminder constantly overshadowing what I was trying to get off the ground. While I wanted her to view Me as her Provider, Medical Provider wasn't exactly what I had in mind.

I could hear a smile in her voice. "i'm well, thank You for asking. i followed up with my primary care physician yesterday and i'm feeling a lot better."

"Good, I'm happy to hear it," I replied, then took a swig of beer.

"That's actually part of the reason why it took me so long to get in touch. i'm swamped at work with a bunch of projects. i had to fly to Italy for a few days and then find the time to fit in a doctor's visit to check on my asthma once i returned. i'm sorry about not calling sooner. i'm normally not this slow to get in touch."

Although I knew what she did for a living, I wanted her to fill Me in on the details. Honestly, I just wanted to hear her voice. I'd been waiting long enough for her to call.

"Understood, and apology accepted. I know what it's like having to deal with a hectic work schedule. So what exactly do you do that has you both swamped and traveling to Italy?"

"i'm an assistant registrar at the Whitney Museum," she replied.

"And that would mean what, exactly?"

she laughed. "Well, as of late, it means i'm the exhibition manager's bitch."

I raised a brow at her statement. Oh, she had a way with words. This conversation was going to be interesting indeed.

"I'm going to need some clarification, because My mind is conjuring up an image I'm fairly certain isn't something you'd do in your place of employment, micah."

she cleared her throat.

Hey, if you open the door, I'm going to walk through it. micah would soon learn that about Me. Don't start what you aren't ready to finish.

"Well, i usually work independently, but we have a new Georgia O'Keeffe exhibit coming in, so i've been the primary contact for a private collector in Italy."

her tone perked up once she began talking about her job. "i've been assisting the exhibition manager with variety of things. i tend to deal with the crating, packing, shipping, and transportation gripes in addition to the insurance aspects."

I could hear a bit of excitement in her voice as her confidence rose. I found it to be an attractive trait. Life is too short to spend time doing things you loathe, especially when it comes to earning a living.

"It's my job to ensure pieces arrive at their destinations safely and return to us intact if we're providing a loan. Everyone is on edge because the curator is a bit of a nut job. i try not to take it out on my staff but some days are tougher than others."

"I see. It sounds stressful. Do you enjoy your job?"

"It's stressful at times, but yes, i absolutely enjoy my job. i adore art, and my occupation not only provides opportunity for me to travel, but it allows my creativity to flow. It's high pressure and high stakes but i'm made for it. i take care of business, but . . ." her pause almost had Me question if she was still on the line until I heard her long sigh. "But it can be a burden sometimes . . . because people expect so much from me."

Interesting. she was used to being everything for everyone, but who took care of her? Who was there for her when she wanted to let go?

"Is that why you're a submissive, micah? Because people expect so much from you? Is being a sub your way of relinquishing control?"

Contrary to popular opinion, submissives do indeed possess a great deal of power. I might be the Dominant one, but a submissive sets the tone for our dynamic. In My eyes, it takes a strong woman to let go and trust her Man will make the best decisions regarding her well-being.

Before I could even think of taking a woman under My wing, I had to know she was secure in herself, that My girl could hold her own. micah seemed strong-willed, which was what attracted Me to her in the first place. There'd been a softness about her, but a flame burned bright underneath the surface. she didn't strike Me as one to let just anyone take the reins—He had to meet her standards.

I knew I had what it took to keep her attention; I wasn't the least bit worried.

she didn't answer My question. Actually, there was an awkward silence that I didn't like one bit. I'd have to revisit that question later on.

"micah?"

"Y-y-yes," she stammered.

"you still with Me, sweetheart?" I asked.

"Yes," she responded softly.

"micah, are you nervous?"

she sighed before answering, "Yes."

"If it makes you feel any better, I'm nervous too." I didn't lie. We hadn't had any of the traditional small talk. I just opened My mouth and blurted out questions she didn't trust Me enough yet to answer.

her muffled scoff was a good sign. At least she hadn't hung up on Me.

"Well, before we get into anything too deep, how about we start with the basics?"

she giggled. "Like what? my favorite color? What's my favorite meal kind of thing?"

her sass was cute and had Me lusting after her.

"I was thinking more along the lines of, are you single?"

"Oh."

Such a simple response but she was giving Me a hard-on in the worst way. "Oh? That's it?"

"Yes. i'm single. i haven't been in a relationship in some time. A string of bad dates, but nothing worthwhile."

Fuck yeah! That's what I wanted to hear.

"One man's failure is My reward," I replied.

"The failure of many men is Your reward." she chuckled. "And what about You, are You single?"

Wait, many men? Say what? "I'm sorry, could you clarify what you meant by 'many men,' micah?"

she let out a small giggle in response to My question. I'm glad she found it amusing, but I wasn't laughing. I wanted clarity. What the fuck did that mean?

"i just meant that i've dated a lot and sadly, many failed when it came to holding my attention. i never seem to find my match and there haven't been many second dates. That's all."

"I see. Well, thank you for the clarification. To answer your question, yes, I'm single. No wife. No girlfriend. No kids. No subs."

"subs?" she asked.

"sub," I corrected. "I only need and want one. I misspoke."

"If i may ask, Rick, how old are You?"

"I'm thirty-seven, sweetheart."

she simply replied with, "Oh."

I couldn't help but laugh. Oh? What the hell did that mean? "Oh" seemed to be her go-to word.

"Don't tell Me I'm too old for you," I said, My tone laced with sarcasm.

"No, not at all. i would not have guessed thirty-seven. You look much younger."

"Why thank you. They say exercise slows down the aging process."

"It certainly looks that way. i'm definitely surprised to hear You say thirty-seven."

she was babbling, and I had so many questions to ask but didn't know where to begin. So I asked what had been on My mind since I learned her name.

"micah?"

"Yes, Rick?"

I loved how she said My name.

"your name is unusual. I can honestly say I've never met a woman named micah. Men yes, but never a woman. What are the origins, if you don't mind Me inquiring?"

"No, I don't mind, and You wouldn't be the first to ask. Based on what my parents have told me, it's actually a variant of Michaela."

"That's pretty too. Feminine."

"Well, long story short, when my mom was little, she had a babysitter named Michaela. She said some of her best childhood memories were the times she spent baking with Michaela and her daughter, Carla."

"That sounds nice. Are you and your mother close?"

"Yes, actually we are. Most of my family lives in California, which can be rough, but yes, my mom and i are close. Peas in a pod, as my dad would say."

I was glad to know that she was close to her family. I came from a tight-knit home, so it was definitely something I wanted My partner to value.

"i guess Michaela had a big enough impact on my mom that she sort of named me after her. 'micah' was my mom's burst of creativity while paying homage to a woman she loved to pieces."

"That's quite an honor to bestow," I replied.

"i agree, but from the stories my mother shared about her childhood, Carla and her family were some of the only white people in their neighborhood who treated her and my grandparents kindly. It was a tough time growing up in the South, so any niceness and generosity was welcomed."

Well, that was deep. I didn't have much in the way of an appropriate response so I let her continue.

"What's funny is when most people meet me in person and they've never seen me or spoken to me over the phone, they're shocked to find out i'm a woman. i'm fairly certain, in ninety-nine-point-nine percent of those cases, they were expecting a guy. In some business settings, i usually go by my middle name, marie, so i don't confuse people."

"I appreciate the insight, micah, and you're definitely all woman. I like the name—it's sexy and unique."

she chuckled. her laughter warmed Me all over.

"Thank You."

I was quite inquisitive when it came to micah and asked an excessive amount of questions, the answers to which I couldn't soak up fast enough. In My professional and personal life, I've come across a fair amount of women who had been all about using their feminine wiles to their advantage. I'd never been so intrigued by a woman before micah. I wanted *this* woman in the worst way.

"micah?"

"Yes, Rick?"

"Do you believe in soul mates?" I asked.

Shit, there I went again just blurting things out, but I wanted to know what she thought about the concept. I believed in a fated connection, and I was beginning to think micah was My soul mate. Our conversation felt right. Everything about tonight felt right. Everything about *her* felt right. I hadn't ever been this enchanted with any other woman.

I was met with a silence that lasted entirely too long for My taste, but she finally spoke up. "i'm not sure. my 'Soul Mate' has probably crossed my path a few times, but maybe He just doesn't see me that way, or maybe the attraction is one-sided. i don't know, i guess part of me wants to think there's someone for everyone, but i don't know. The world is a big place. If you throw the D/s aspect into the equation, it becomes virtually impossible to think a match exists."

Hmm, so she wasn't a fan of Fate. I'd have to convince her.

"Even if it's a meeting in passing, micah, your Soul Mate will find a way. If the connection is strong enough, He'll find you. He'll always find you. If a Man deems a woman worthy, He will make her His. He will fight for her. He will honor her. He will provide for her. He will protect her. I believe paths are meant to cross at certain points in time. People meet each when they're supposed to. It's what the universe wants."

I put all My cards on the table. I'm sure the shit I laid out scared her, but she wasn't the only one who was scared. I may be direct, but dating and messing around had long ago lost their appeal.

Shit. My biological clock was ticking too, and Fate, she was a clever girl, literally dropping My heart's desires into My lap—I couldn't be more grateful. I wanted to explore this, but Mine weren't the only feelings to consider.

Once again, the silence was deafening.

In a tone that was barely audible, she asked Me a question I hadn't anticipated. "What do You want from me, Rick?"

Well, so much for pretenses and talk of doing what the universe wanted. she asked the million-dollar question, and I wasn't quite sure how I should respond. How do You tell a woman You want *everything* without freaking her the fuck out?

Our interaction up to that point had been limited, and we were in the early stages, but I knew what I wanted. I wanted to claim her. I wanted to fuck her. I wanted to love her.

People often say that when Cupid's arrow strikes, the little bastard zooms in on your heart with sniper-like accuracy. With micah, he hit his target and was now Riverdancing on My heart. I'm not the type to believe in love at first sight, but there was something different about micah marie foster.

I steeled Myself and let go. No sense in putting on a façade. she asked a direct question so she'd get a direct answer. "I want everything, micah. I'm willing to go at your pace, but I want everything. I'm looking for *her*: My obedient vixen, My lover, My friend, My wife, My everything."

I could hear her breathing heavily on the other end of the line. My God, I didn't want to send her into another asthma attack. "sweetheart, I'm not trying to freak you out. I'm sorry, but I'm simply being honest."

"Okay . . ."

"I want you, micah. Will you give us a chance?"

she took a deep breath that apparently calmed us both, because after that she opened up like a blossom in the morning sun, and I sank back onto My sofa and basked in her fragrant warmth.

After her initial hesitation, we talked about any and everything from politics, to television, to what we were seeking in a partner. The conversation was effortless. she made Me laugh, I made her laugh, and we ended up chatting until almost five in the morning.

This might have been a little fast for her taste, but I invited her to My condo the following night for that drink I had promised. Shit, she made Me wait more than two weeks to even hear her voice again. Asking her to My apartment shouldn't be that big of a deal, but I knew she was the play-it-safe type.

I wanted to see her. I *needed* to see her. So I offered to cook her dinner to sweeten the deal.

i was tired. Dog tired. i stayed up until the wee hours of the morning chatting on the phone with Rick and had absolutely no regrets. Well, not until i had to drag my ass into work and deal with Joan.

Thank goodness for coffee, because it was the only reason i presented as human. Even zombies would've been scared of me.

Once Rick expressed genuine interest in me, i felt comfortable enough to share my feelings with Him.

He wanted to know my story. He wanted to know why i chose to be a submissive, how long i'd been in the lifestyle, what type of dynamic i was seeking, what type of Dom. He interviewed me just as much as i interviewed Him.

No one had ever cared to know the reasons behind my submission, so Rick's interest was a welcome change. The Men i had served preferred temporary arrangements. i never quite clicked with anyone enough to want something more out of our situation, so walking away when things had run their course had never been difficult.

i was looking forward to seeing Him again, though. Under normal circumstances, i would never agree to meet a Man i hadn't known for an extended period of time at His apartment for dinner and drinks.

my creep-o-meter was dialed down to zero. Rick didn't give off an ounce of crazypants. To be on the safe side, i told kisa where i was headed. Armed with His address and telephone number, plus His place of employment, kisa's "i've got my eye on You" arsenal was locked and loaded.

my best friend was skeptical. she didn't think Rick was a jerk or a sexual predator or anything like that—she was merely looking out for my best interest, which i appreciated. we both had experienced our fair share of poseurs, so she armed me with a brand-new canister of pepper spray and told me to be extra careful.

Rick had been expecting me. The door attendant barely gave me an opportunity to identify myself before calling up to Rick to announce my arrival. i chuckled at kisa's warning and the enthusiastic greeting i received as i pressed the button for Rick's floor.

i fidgeted and pulled down my bandage dress while the elevator carried me to the twenty-fifth floor. When i was home and in front of my bedroom mirror, it seemed like a good idea to wear the skintight navy dress and canary-yellow peep-toe stilettos. Although the dress stopped at my upper thigh, i worried now that it barely covered my ass. One thing was for certain: i was going to give the good Doctor a show.

i'm not sure what my plan of action was, other than to look as appealing as possible.

The last time Rick saw me, i was being discharged from the hospital wearing a pair of distressed jeans with my hair pulled back in an unruly ponytail. Tonight i wanted Him to have a different image, so i spent more time than usual on my hair and makeup. Of course, i was nervous, so i proceeded to bite my lower lip, but stopped when i remembered i was wearing lipstick.

If my lipstick was going to be ruined, it wouldn't be my own doing.

i was poised to ring the bell when Rick opened the door.

He stood leaning against the door frame looking the part of a Greek god, wearing a pair of black dress slacks and a light blue shirt with the sleeves rolled up to His elbows. He appeared both dapper and casual, and if i was being truthful, mouthwatering. The glasses perched upon Rick's nose made Him resemble a beefier version of Clark Kent. Not a bad image to have, since Clark was all sorts of yum.

He gently took my hand, leading me over the threshold and into His apartment.

"Hi, micah. you look absolutely breathtaking. Welcome to My home," He said, closing and locking the door behind us.

i'm pretty sure i blushed at His compliment. Well, my cheeks felt warm and my heart felt like it was about to pop out of my chest.

"Hi, Rick. Thank You," i replied.

Rick spun me around to get a full view of the piece of thread i called a dress. i think He approved.

His eyes settled on my breasts before He spoke. "you have to know that it's going to be difficult for Me to focus this evening when you're wearing something so incredibly flattering."

i knew what He meant; i anticipated Him having the same problem.

His eyes lingered on my chest a little longer than necessary. i was fairly certain He was enjoying the view. Tonight, no push-up bra was needed; the dress enhanced *all* of my assets. *Dangerous curves ahead.*

i cleared my throat. "i'm sorry, is it too much?"

"No, pretty girl. you look stunning."

Something about the way He called me "pretty girl" gave me butterflies.

He once again linked His fingers with mine, leading me farther into His condo. The place was spacious and immaculate with a modern but contemporary décor. i'm not sure what i expected, but somehow i knew this Man would have impeccable taste. His condo also provided an amazing view overlooking Central Park. i could only imagine how much the annual fees set Him back.

This was one of those instances where i felt like i was out of my league. i held my own professionally and financially, but even so, my apartment was located in Spanish Harlem, not Central Park West. This side of the park was explicitly relegated to the upper echelon of New Yorkers. i was doing well, but clearly not as well as Rick. How could He afford such a spacious condo on a doctor's salary? Doctors are well-off, but not this well-off.

After giving me a tour of His apartment, Rick and i settled in the kitchen. He pulled out my chair and waited for me to be seated before He poured me a glass of wine. As i sipped my wine, He filled our plates with the chicken stir-fry and wild rice He had prepared. It was great to see that there were still Men who believed in chivalry.

"Do You cook often?" i asked, taking another sip of the Pinot Grigio He had selected.

He placed our plates on the table and took a seat across from me. "Define 'often,'" He countered.

"Well, You're a Bachelor. i was wondering if You eat out of takeout containers more often than preparing home-cooked meals?"

He picked up His fork and took a few bites, making me wait for His response.

He wiped His mouth with a napkin and paused for a moment before speaking. "I don't cook often, but if I do, it's usually something quick and lean like what we're eating now." Rick rested His elbows on the table and leaned forward. "With My schedule, by the time I arrive home I'm not in the mood to stand over a hot stove. It's times like that where I'd really enjoy domestic servitude. I would come home and My girl would have My dinner waiting."

Domestic servitude didn't bother me one bit. i enjoyed it, since i was a bit of a neat freak. Everything in my apartment had a place. i think the term for someone who's into apartment therapy coupled with a bit of obsessive compulsiveness is a "domestic goddess." i might've heard it mentioned on one of those HGTV design shows, or maybe it was *Queer Eye for the Straight Guy*, but don't quote me on that.

Providing for a Dom in a capacity that made His life easier was my duty. If that meant doing His laundry, making His meals, keeping His home clean, so be it. Besides, cleaning was therapeutic for me. It was yet another way i dealt with stress.

i took a few more bites of the sweet and tangy stir-fry. Rick had a few skills in the kitchen.

"Is domestic servitude something you're interested in, micah?" He asked.

"Yes, Sir. i consider myself a bit of a neat freak. Although i've never been in a long-term arrangement, i've served as house girl for other Doms in the past," i replied.

He quirked an eyebrow and stared at me . . . *hard*.

i immediately stopped eating and put my fork down, trying to replay my last few words in my head. Did i overstep my bounds and say something inappropriate by discussing previous Doms? Why was He looking at me like that?

"you called Me 'Sir.'"

Yep, i'm pretty sure my cheeks were flushed. While i may be of a darker hue, i felt as if my entire face had turned bright red. For all i knew, i was giving that damn reindeer Rudolph a run for his money.

"i-i'm sorry. i—"

He interrupted my stammering. "micah. It's all right. I prefer you address Me that way, but I wanted it to come naturally."

i didn't know what to say. i addressed Him as Sir as if it were the norm. i had gotten caught up in our discussion and it . . . it just happened.

"Between our phone conversation and the time we've spent together tonight talking, it's pretty obvious we have something powerful between us, but we've got to feel each other and see how well we jive. What works, what doesn't. I want you to be comfortable with Me. I accept you addressing Me as Sir."

In my nervousness, i lightly chewed on my lower lip. He seemed so incredibly calm while i was a mess inside. i lowered my eyes to focus on my plate and poked at a piece of chicken with my fork.

He reached across the table and gently lifted my chin, pinning me with His gaze. "Hey, pretty girl, we still have a bit more ground to cover. We only scratched the surface over the phone. Tonight, we dive in."

my heart chose that moment to beat erratically against my chest. i was intrigued by Him. i don't think He realized i noticed that was the second time He called me "pretty girl." i liked it. i liked it very much. Something about Rick made me want to be *His* pretty girl.

Dinner progressed well. To Me, micah was a gem. A beautiful diamond that had yet to be adequately polished and displayed.

Aside from her stunning physical attributes, I found her to be intelligent, enterprising, cultured, artistic, and funny. Our conversations flowed after we got over the initial awkwardness; it was like we had known each other for years.

We talked during dinner, and when micah laughed her face completely lit up. Beautiful.

Watching micah laugh made Me happier than I'd been in years.

Remember I said I don't date? It's true. Once My last partner and I parted, I had no interest in getting emotionally involved with another woman. I found women to fulfill My sexual needs and that was it. Bed 'em and keep it moving. I didn't want to go down that path again: emotionally investing in someone only to have them fuck up what we had. I thought samantha was satisfied, but it turns out My lifestyle wasn't what she wanted long-term.

samantha was My live-in submissive. We were together for about two years before she decided to call it quits without any warning. she gave no indication that she was unhappy, just a brief conversation after work one day that ended in her telling Me she was leaving.

There was a time when I was angry with sam for leaving, since she knew what she had signed up for from the beginning. All the anger and animosity I held withered away a long time ago. I let that shit go. Harboring ill will could only bring You down.

After that fiasco, I'd been gun-shy about becoming emotionally vulnerable with another woman. But until two weeks ago, no one had sparked My interest long enough to make Me think about the future. My perspective had changed. samantha was simply a road I had to cross to get to My present opportunity: micah. Enough time had passed and I was ready to start over.

We needed to expand our discussion of limits we began on the phone, so I clicked the shuffle button on the stereo and led micah to the sofa as Miles Davis's album *Kind of Blue* filtered through the condo.

micah leaned back against the sofa and crossed her legs. her dress steadily climbed up her thigh as she shifted in her seat. her skin shimmered and I couldn't help but stare. There is nothing more attractive to Me than a woman with flawless skin.

I sat in an armchair, thinking of all the dirty shit I wanted to do to her. Goddamn, she was sweeter than pie. Maybe it was the two and a half glasses of wine we consumed during dinner, but watching her as she spoke turned Me on. I wasn't drunk or buzzed, but I was feeling full of energy. It wasn't anything she did or said, but My overwhelming desire for her. We were discussing micah's hard limits when I removed My glasses and placed them on the coffee table.

"i'm not into race play of any sort, verbal or physical degradation, scening with anyone under twenty-one, bestiality, fisting, or bodily fluids."

"I see," I replied. "Anything else you wish to add?"

"No, Sir. Those are my absolute hard limits."

micah maintained eye contact momentarily before dropping her gaze to My glasses on the coffee table. her teeth once again grazed her bottom lip as she shifted on the sofa.

I was beginning to think micah was full of nervous energy, and I have to say, I took great pleasure in her attempt to control her demeanor while she spoke.

she raised her eyes to Mine and continued. "i'm flexible. While many things may not be my cup of tea, i think it's good for a sub and her Dom to explore. her boundaries are pushed because she trusts Him not to do anything to harm her emotionally or physically."

I rose up from the chair and walked over to where micah sat. her eyes intently focused on My towering form until I was so close that she was forced to lean back to meet My gaze. I extended My hand and she took it without delay. she was a good girl, such a good girl, displaying obedience without the slightest hesitation.

I pulled her up from the sofa a bit more roughly than I intended, but I didn't regret it. her body pressed firmly against My chest. Fuck, she smelled amazing. I placed My hands on the small of her back, just slightly above the curve of her ass, and nuzzled against her ear.

It was clear from the sigh that escaped her lips, micah was feeling some kind of way about Me. she was turned on, and that was good. Very good.

I whispered in her ear, "My hard limit is sharing. I do not share under any circumstances, micah. What's Mine is Mine, so that puts a damper on your threesome plans."

Even though micah had an unfulfilled fantasy, and I was all about meeting My woman's needs, there was no way I was going to let another Man fuck My pretty girl. she was Mine. And her pussy was Mine. I share many things, but pussy was never one of them.

"I'm also in agreement with your other hard limits," I said as My breath caused tiny goose bumps to rise along micah's neck and jaw.

she tried to wriggle out of My grasp, but I wanted her to feel what she did to Me. There was no way to hide My erection.

I let her out of My embrace, offering My hand to her once more. she didn't make eye contact, which disappointed Me, but she did take My hand.

"When I gave you the tour of My condo, micah, I neglected to show you one room in particular: My playroom. Would you like to see it?"

she nodded without hesitation. In that moment, she looked coy, demure, wanting, eager. I wanted a taste every ounce of her.

We had briefly discussed the possibility of play when we'd spoken on the phone, but nothing was set in stone. I think she and I were on the same page tonight, though. I wanted her in that room—she belonged there and she knew it.

More than anything, I wanted to kiss her. Those lush lips of hers were calling out to Me and I wanted to devour them. Throughout the evening, I'd witnessed a variety of smiles from micah. When she laughed and lit up, that was by far My favorite.

I interlaced micah's fingers with Mine and made a path down the corridor toward My sanctuary. For the past couple of years, I only played at clubs like Spanxxx or private parties. I hadn't brought a woman to My playroom in five long years. I missed sharing My special place with a special lady—My special lady.

Showtime.

micah

The music pulsing through the sound system gave me chills. "Flamenco Sketches" provided the soundtrack of the moment. He was a Miles Davis fan. There was no way for Him to know, but *Kind of Blue* was my favorite album by the trumpeter. It's one of those must-have albums for a jazz enthusiast.

The musical taste of most men i'd dated recently was questionable. i was starting to believe the art of seduction via love songs had died, but Rick had me rethinking my stance.

Music was the gateway to the soul. It conveyed what words alone could not; it seemed that Rick understood that. His musical selection was perfect. The soft tapping of the drums. The purr of the saxophone and trombone. The quiet plink of the piano. The riffing, the trills, the chords all flowed around my eardrums like warm caramel.

His song choice selection told me He was the kind of Man who liked to take His time. my stomach continued to do flips as He took my hand and led me down the dimly lit corridor. i got the feeling He was about to turn my world upside down.

He stopped in front of a door i had pegged as the laundry room during the initial tour and pulled a lone key from His pants pocket. He unlocked the door and entered ahead of me into the darkened space, and then switched on the lights.

i was immediately struck by the view. The twinkling lights of Midtown Manhattan illuminated the room through panoramic floor-to-ceiling windows. Times Square sparkled in the distance as Rick fiddled with the dimmer on the wall. Softer lighting cast a smooth glow over the room. This was His playroom, where He was most Himself.

Wow. He must really, really like me.

my gaze was fixed on the view of the city when Rick filled my line of sight.

"We're high enough up, but the windows are made of privacy glass." His lip pulled up on one side to reveal a deep dimple. "In case you were uncomfortable."

This Man just got better and better.

He turned and moved to the window. His muscles rippled under His clothing when He reached for the pulley to close the drapes.

my God. This was unreal.

"Feel free to look around," He said from His position at the window while my eyes adjusted to the dim lighting.

"Thank You, Sir." i could feel His eyes on me, watching my every move.

One wall showcased a variety of floggers and paddles and chains hanging from hooks. my gaze lifted to the ceiling, where more hooks were located. This space did not belong to a Man who simply had a hobby. Rick took His play seriously. Very seriously.

i ran my hand along the spanking bench, but my attention was on the Saint Andrew's Cross.

my thoughts shifted back and forth between worry and inadequacy as my eyes landed on a rattan cane leaning against the wall where the floggers were housed.

Rick wrapped His hands around my waist, pulling me out of my thoughts by leaning His sculpted frame against my back. He was a giant compared to me. Even in these heels, Rick easily dwarfed me. They say size doesn't matter, but with Rick, size was everything, and i felt everything pressing up against me. He ran His nose across my jaw and back again, His stubble raising goosebumps on my skin with each pass. And then His lips were on my flesh. Hot. Wet. Firm but supple.

"I've finally got you where I've wanted you for the longest time," He whispered just behind my ear.

i wasn't having an asthma attack, but i couldn't breathe.

Rick moaned against my neck, latching on, swirling His tongue along my skin, followed by wet, open-mouthed kisses. "I hadn't wanted to bring a woman in here until I met you."

It was a miracle i was still standing because i was pretty sure i was dreaming.

He opened His hand wide, palming my belly and pressing me against Him even more. "I'm very serious about making you Mine, micah."

Arousal and terror had me trembling at Rick's hand.

He spun me around so we were face to face. i bit my lip, wanting to say or do something that would quiet the storm in Rick's eyes.

"Goddamn," He moaned before kissing me. i'd been longing for this moment, waiting for the warmth of His mouth to stake its claim, and He delivered.

The gentle brush of His lips against mine became more firm, more insistent. He devoured me whole. i sighed, luxuriating in the perfection of Rick's touch. The deep flavors of the wine lingered on His tongue, making me crave more of Him. His hand held me at the top of my neck and His fingers tangled in the hair at my nape. Rick's other hand gripped the hem of my dress. He alternated between sucking on my bottom lip and swirling His tongue around mine.

Music and moans filled the room. Miles hit a high note and Rick pressed me harder against His hips. my hands flew to His hair and shoulder at the feel of Him; i would soon be on the verge of an orgasm if Rick kept up His taunting. How is it that a kiss could feel this good? Every bit of Him, from His tongue to His fingertips, sent tingles down my spine and made my head spin. Damn.

Experiencing an emotional connection with someone could be scary. It was overwhelming, especially when the other person was doing everything within His power to make me to fall for Him. If He kept kissing me like that, Rick wouldn't have to work too hard before i would be completely smitten.

Why does "smitten" have a romantic connotation when its root word means "to knock down"? i guess that's what falling in lo— Reluctantly, i pulled away, breaking the kiss and then turning from Him.

my thoughts were a jumbled mess, and i didn't like feeling so out of control. On one hand, i wanted more of Him; on the other hand, things were happening too fast. my life had become a cliché—

this moment had all the thrilling terror of a roller coaster ride, and i did not want it to stop until it was truly over. As long as Rick was at the controls, i never wanted this ride to stop.

So why did i feel like this was wrong? my eyes wrenched shut and i crossed my arms over my chest, holding on to my shoulders.

i had traveled past Butterflyville and found myself lost in Queasyland. Would i be enough? Was i what He truly wanted? Although i had never been owned, i had played often over the years. But would my limited experience be enough to live up to His standards?

my lungs burned. He placed a finger under my chin and tilted my head up. i opened my eyes and released a long breath. There was nothing i could do but confront His scrutiny.

"Is My pretty girl unhappy?" He asked.

"N-no, Sir. i'm okay." i'm sure He didn't believe me.

Rick bent to meet my eyes. "micah, one thing I will always ask is that you speak the truth even if you think I'll disapprove. It's okay to feel how you do—I feel it too." He pulled my hands down and held them in His, never taking His deep blue eyes off my face. "you're scared because you're feeling emotionally vulnerable. your body is responding to Me, but your thoughts are swirling in different directions."

There'd never been an issue before. But with Rick, the distance i'd put between my body and my heart disappeared, and i was on the verge of freaking the fuck out.

"you don't have to be afraid—not of Me." He rubbed His thumb over my bottom lip and tugged, prying it from between my teeth. "It's kind of hard to concentrate when you do that. . . ." He continued to stroke my lip while He spoke. "I'm here with you, micah. We're both taking a risk."

"We have to trust each other," i said in barely a whisper.

"Exactly." He pulled away from me and began unbuttoning His shirt, then tossed it onto the bondage table.

Sweet heavenly Father, i found it difficult to tear my eyes away from His sculpted torso. All of that was hidden underneath a lab coat? i figured He'd spent a lot of time in the gym, but the Man was so physically attractive that my lips quivered. Rick's physique was, in a word, impressive.

"Do you want to do this, micah?" One side of His face lifted into a sly smile and raised eyebrow.

i wanted to kiss that smug look off His face. He seemed to enjoy me standing there ogling Him and drooling like a doofus.

"We can stop if you want. It won't change anything. Our evening can take a different path, and that's perfectly fine with Me. you control what happens here. I move at your pace."

He took a risk by welcoming me into His sanctuary. If i wanted something real, i had to take a risk, too. What if Rick was the catalyst for lasting change in my life?

"There's absolutely no pressure for you to do anything you're not comfortable with. you tell Me, pretty girl, what do you want?"

He stood in front of me, leaning against the spanking bench with His arms crossed against His hulking chest, awaiting my response.

i allowed my gaze to linger on the implements hanging from the wall. What did i want? i wanted to break down walls. i wanted to step outside of my comfort zone. i wanted to say good-bye to temporary arrangements. i wanted to be with Him in this space. Most of all, i wanted to explore this connection Rick and i shared. What if this was the start of something? i wanted to let go with Him and only Him.

"Yes, Sir, i want to give this a shot."

He nodded. "Very well," He replied with a sly grin. Clearly, He was pleased by my response.

"What's your safe word, micah?" He asked as i stared at His well-defined chest.

my eyes continued to trail down His chest, stopping at His midsection. *Abs for days*. Of course, i would have a one-track mind. Rick was exceedingly attractive in all His shirtless glory, but He didn't strike me as the type to bank on His physical appeal. i was glad. He was so much more than a pretty face.

"'Cookie,' Sir," i blurted out, shifting in my heels.

He laughed. "Cookie? Hmm, interesting choice. Cute. Very cute."

"So, no race play, no verbal or physical degradation, no play with anyone under twenty-one—which is irrelevant, since I don't share—no animals, no fisting, no bodily fluids. I'm assuming you mean piss, shit, and blood, is that correct?

"Yes, You're correct," i responded.

His tone was different—it was very much the tone He held when i was His patient and He rattled off questions regarding my medical history. He was in Doctor mode.

"Am I missing anything as far as your hard limits are concerned, micah?" He slowly circled me. Studying me. Examining me.

i remained still and kept my eyes downcast, unsure of what i should do next. "No, Sir, that's all for now."

"How much do you like that dress?" He asked.

"i like it very much, Sir. It fits me like a glove and cost a pretty penny."

"you do wear it well. I'm rather fond of it Myself, so I promise not to tear it. I would like to see you wear it for Me again," He said, gently running His fingers along my collarbone as He continued to circle me.

He was so close.

He briefly paused to stand in front of me and i shivered. my eyes traveled upward, landing on His pecs when they twitched before He once again moved out of my line of sight. The proximity of His body, His voice, His scent . . . heady.

He stood behind me with His body flush against mine. The weight and warmth of His hands on my shoulders brought a whimper to my throat. Rick ghosted a hand down my arm and removed my bangles from my wrist, placing them on the bondage table beside us.

He then lifted my arm over my head, tugging the dress zipper down partway. Rick silently manipulated my arms so He could pull the top of my dress down past my shoulders, freeing my breasts. He lowered the zipper all the way, letting my dress pool at my waist.

Cupping my breasts, He leaned in, pressing His cheek to mine as He gently caressed and kneaded my deep brown flesh. The pressure increased and Rick ran His rough thumbs over my nipples before pinching and flicking them.

There was no way to contain the moans Rick drew out of me. He had barely touched me, and i was already unraveling. While i was somewhat scared of the unknown, my brain was far more concerned with His unyielding hands on my breasts.

"you have the most beautiful breasts, micah. They're pert and respond so well to Me. I love the size of your nipples. I'm going to enjoy sucking on them."

my head fell back against His shoulder and my nipples stood at attention. His touch changed from barely there to almost painful as He continued to tease me. Repeated moans escaped my lips, and i soon found myself biting my tongue so i wouldn't get louder.

He released my breasts without warning, and the warmth of His chest no longer caressed my back. He took my hand and guided me across the room toward the Saint Andrew's Cross.

"How are you with orgasm control, micah? Can you handle it?" He asked with a devilish twinkle in His eyes.

"i've done it before, Sir, although i can't say that my experience is extensive. If i'm trained to Your specifications, i'm sure i can come when asked. But it will take some time, Sir."

"Good answer," He said, smiling.

He led me to the Saint Andrew's Cross and extended my hands above my head so that i was restrained to the Cross. "How do your hands feel?" He asked securing the restraint against my right hand.

"Good, Sir, this is good," i replied, wiggling my fingers to test the tightness of the bonds. Seemingly satisfied by my comfort, He ran His hand down my arm and across my body. my breathing sped up and my flesh tingled under His touch.

He looked directly into my eyes as He spoke. "I want you, micah. I want to own all of you. I want your heart, your soul, your spirit, your pussy . . . everything."

Why did He want me? No one had ever been so blatant with their intentions. This was finally what i had been seeking, but why did it scare me so damn much? i managed a smile although i was feeling all sorts of confusing emotions.

"Why? Why me?" i couldn't get away or cover myself if i tried. On display, i was completely vulnerable. If He chose to hurt me, i doubted my heart could recover. But there was a sincerity in His eyes that made me want to believe Him more than i'd ever wanted anything else in the world.

This wasn't a game. Taking on a submissive wasn't some flight of fancy for Rick. This was His life, and He played for keeps.

He grabbed my chin, forcing me to keep His stare. "I told you, micah, I want it all. you're beautiful," He said as His lips grazed my cheek. "you're intelligent." He pressed His lips against my other cheek. "you complement Me."

i was expecting Him to kiss my mouth, but instead He stepped away from me with a stern look in His eyes. "And you kept Me waiting."

"But i explained! my job—" i tugged at my restraints.

Rick's laughter rumbled through the room. "And you're oh so feisty. I think that's what I like best about you, pretty girl."

my shoulders slumped as best they could in my present position. "So You're not upset?"

"Not terribly, no. I have you now. We'll just have to make up for lost time. Are you still agreeable to our present course?"

i nodded.

"God blessed you with a delectable mouth, micah. Please use it."

Shit. And my naturally smart mouth was going to get me into a lot of trouble with Him. It'd been a while since i'd been in a scene with someone with so much authority. i didn't want to let Rick down, but then again, a little punishment had its own rewards.

"i'm sorry. i'm out of practice, Sir. Yes, i would like to continue with whatever You have planned."

Rick checked my bindings again, this time pressing His entire body against mine. He released a contented moan in my ear. "While I want all of you, what I crave most of all right now is to hear you come for Me."

After His bold statement, He made His way toward a chest of drawers across the room, slowly opening the top drawer, then pulling out a piece of paper.

"Here's a copy of My recent test results. I have a clean bill of health, micah."

He held the document up for me to read, since my hands were restrained. my eyes scanned the STD panel. Each test had "negative" beside it. He'd had this done two weeks ago, according to the date at the top of the page.

"I always complete a panel when I begin a new sexual relationship, so I had this panel done a few days after you were discharged. It was overly ambitious of Me, but because I'm a physician, I know how important these things are. Safety should always come first."

Really now? He went and had an STD panel done after i was discharged? He was certainly sure of Himself, and that aggravated me.

"And in case you're wondering, I last had sex a month ago. I can get tested again in another two months if you prefer, but I'm not having sexual relations with anyone. It'll just be you. I promise I'm monogamous, micah."

He stood in front of me with an impassioned look on His face.

That was pretty damn presumptuous of Him. If this had been any other Guy, i likely would've handed His ass to Him. Honestly, part of me was thrilled that He was so responsible, however, another part of me was focused on the scope of what He'd done.

He plotted this. He planned this. i didn't think He did it to be malicious. Again, there was no creepy vibe, just a Guy hell-bent on getting what He wanted. And what He wanted was for me to let my guard down. i was willing to explore and let my guard down tonight, but He was thinking bigger picture—much bigger. And He had been from the beginning.

i nodded when i was done reading. i wasn't sure how to process what i'd just learned. i could always tell Him that i'd changed my mind, but my curiosity was getting the better of me. i could end this at any time. For now, i'd let it play out a little longer.

"Do you have any questions for Me?" He asked, walking over to the chest of drawers and returning the paperwork.

"When would You like me to get tested, Sir?"

He smirked. "That's the beauty of My unique position. Because of My occupation, I have access to your results from last year. Have you had any form of sex in the last three months?"

"No, Sir, the last time i was with someone intimately was a year ago."

"Then your results from your last panel are sufficient," He replied. His lips pursed and the corners of His eyes crinkled as if He were fighting a smile.

So He was happy i wasn't getting laid? i wasn't. i couldn't do the casual sex thing. The main reason i hadn't been with anyone intimately is because i sought something substantial. But i got the feeling He knew that. Obviously, He wanted to be the One to change it.

"Are you currently on any form of birth control?" He inquired.

i was exposed, literally and figuratively. Aside from my dress, which was hitched up around my waist, i was practically naked. The thong and the heels i wore while He scrutinized my sexual history and methods of birth control weren't helpful in shielding me from an inquisition.

He didn't exactly take things slow. Then again, i was bound to a Saint Andrew's Cross in my skivvies, so i wasn't moving at a snail's pace either, but i couldn't help the snarky reply that escaped my lips. "You mean to tell me You didn't see that bit of info in my medical history too? Or did You not look?" i guess i was a little more than mildly annoyed.

He raised a brow, halting mere inches from my face. His breathing was a bit erratic—i had pissed Him off.

i inhaled sharply. Now was not the time for me to be bratty.

His stony expression indicated He was not pleased with my smarting off. He attempted to pull my dress up to cover my breasts before reaching above my head and releasing my right hand from the restraints.

"Wait, w-what are You doing?" i asked.

"I'm sorry, micah, I'm going too fast, we should stop. you're annoyed. I'm annoyed. We shouldn't do this. Let's try to—"

"No, wait," i said, interrupting Him. Things couldn't end like this. Although my response was a defense mechanism, i shouldn't have responded that way. "i should be apologizing. i responded rudely. i'm sorry, Sir."

"micah, when I ask you a question, your response should be 'Yes, Sir,' 'No, Sir,' et cetera. I don't want to hear any sort of back talk. Do we understand each other?"

"Y-yes, Sir."

"If you're not ready for something or you want Me to slow down, tell Me. I need you to communicate with Me, okay?" He said, placing my wrist back into the restraint.

"Are we good now?" He inquired.

"Yes, Sir."

"Good girl. Now, let's try again. Are you on any birth control?"

"No, Sir."

"Well, micah, that's about to change. When I said Mine, I meant it. I'm only interested in exclusivity. What's your preferred method of birth control?"

"i've been on the Pill previously, Sir, and i have no problems starting a low dose. i used to take Alesse."

"Good girl. Schedule an appointment with your gynecologist as soon as possible to get a prescription. I could write you a script for a low dosage oral contraceptive, but I want to be sure that, with your asthma, we don't overload your system by introducing too many new medications. your gynecologist is more familiar with your health history and reactions to meds."

"Yes, Sir."

Rick silently knelt in front of me and pushed my dress down my body until He was lifting my foot to remove it all the way. He tossed it onto the bondage table where His shirt lay.

i gasped, not expecting His move. One moment He was ready to release me, the next He was removing my clothing.

Where would this go? i wanted us to rekindle what we were starting. Clearly, He wanted the same thing.

"I don't want any barriers between us, micah," He commented while pushing my thong aside and sliding His fingers up and down the slick slit of my pussy.

i'm not sure if He was referring to my thong or condoms when He said that, but i had the feeling He meant both.

"Mmm. you're very wet for Me."

i moaned at His touch.

That must've done something to Him, because in a swift move, He tore the flimsy material from my body. i was now fully nude, except for my canary-yellow heels.

There was something primal about me being fully exposed while He still wore His slacks and shoes. His bare chest was as close as i would get to skin-to-skin contact.

"I saved the dress as promised, but the thong was a casualty," He said while gingerly parting my pussy lips with His fingers.

my clit peeked out from its hiding place, waiting for His mouth to extend a proper hello.

His eyes were hooded and filled with desire as He gazed up at me. "micah, there are rules. you do not come unless I say so. If you come, I will punish you, and it will not be pleasant. If you think this is torture, punishment for disobeying Me isn't any better. Do you understand?"

i nodded.

"Do you understand?" He repeated.

"Y-yes, Sir."

"Use your safe word if at any time you feel it necessary."

i couldn't give a proper response before He lifted both my legs over His shoulders, my ass resting against the Saint Andrew's Cross and my arms suspended above me from the restraints, aligning my pussy with His mouth.

The moment of contact was like an inferno. i bucked, but He held me in place, spreading my legs wider for greater access. His tongue probed my pussy lips like a Man feasting on His last meal. He licked and sucked my pearl with the perfect amount of intensity and tenderness.

The pleasure, oh God, the pleasure was overpowering.

His impeccable tongue technique had tears slowly falling from my eyes. Alternating between slow, grueling licks and fast strokes brought me to the brink of release.

my orgasm forced its way to the surface, but i tried my best to keep it at bay. Not once, not twice, but three times i fought it off. Each time i thought i had succeeded, He did something to force a guttural scream from my lips. He finger-fucked me, hitting my G-spot twice using a come-hither motion while still inside me.

Many women fantasized about a Man who knew her body well, but me? i was cursing my body's response to Him. Rick seemed to know my body *too well*, and my body rebelled against me to play by His rules instead.

By the fourth attempt, i was too weak to put up a decent fight. The orgasm rolled through me with such force that i screamed as i released. Once the last of the spasms ceased, my exhausted body went limp.

He slowly removed my legs from His shoulders and lowered them to the floor before rising to His full height. He removed a handkerchief from His back pocket, wiping His mouth of my essence.

i didn't dare look at Him, but i could feel His eyes on me. i knew He was disappointed in me. i was disappointed in myself. i tried hard to fight the pleasure but couldn't.

He knew it too.

He anticipated my failure on some level. It was a game to Him.

i wasn't seasoned enough to control my orgasms.

He knew i'd fail and He was testing me.

"A decadent and spicy blend of peach with a hint of cinnamon. you are delectable, micah. I can definitely get used to the taste of your pussy. It is a treat.

"Did you know you were a squirter, pretty girl? you ejaculated in My mouth. It's been a long while since I've been with a squirter. Thank you for reminding Me of what I've been missing and showing Me what I have to look forward to."

i was embarrassed by His last comment. While i was far from a prude, i was mortified that i'd squirted in His mouth. i had only done that with one other partner.

If i didn't know better, i'd think He was smiling, but i still couldn't look at Him. i wouldn't look at Him despite Rick sounding pleased by what happened.

i tried not to dwell on it too much, but i was also afraid of what would happen next—i came when He explicitly forbade me not to. i stared at my brightly colored heels and rubbed my knees together, making the stickiness between my thighs worse.

"you also shave your pussy, which is nice, but I prefer you wax from here on out. But enough about that—we can revisit likes, dislikes, and preferences later."

"you broke the rules, micah. you came without permission. Remarkably, you resisted a few times, which was good, but not good enough. Are you ready to accept your punishment?"

i nodded and whispered, "Yes, Sir."

Rick was intense and exacting in everything He said and did. i was curious yet scared to see what would come next. Would this be a pleasurable experience or an unbearable one?

"Good girl."

Still coming down from one of the most intense orgasms i had ever experienced, my mind was hazy, my eyes glassy and hooded. Euphoria cleared and His words began to replay in my mind.

Are you ready to accept your punishment?

Orgasm denial was always something i failed at. i mean really, who could say they were skilled at *not* coming? It's not like orgasm denial was an Olympic event, but it did require dedicated conditioning and training; i had never been with a Dom long enough for my body to adapt to His demands.

Trying not to come was hard work. Denying yourself pleasure when it was within your grasp was extremely difficult, but you did it because you knew it was pleasurable for your Dominant.

Rick went through drawers and pulled out various implements i assumed He intended to use on me. If He was trying to intimidate me, it was working. i clenched my thighs together.

"micah, you looked so beautiful coming for Me, but you were told to withstand the pleasure," He said before walking over to me and placing a black blindfold over my eyes.

Once the blindfold was in place, i was engulfed by Him.

His hands lingered in my hair and on my face, His digits smelling of me, before moving lower, stopping to fondle my breasts, then cup the pulsating flesh between my thighs. Stubble, soft lips, and hot, moist breath grazed my skin, following the trail His hands forged down my body before lingering at my ankles.

The slight pinch and pull of my skin as He secured my legs in the restraints shocked me out of my Rick-induced haze.

i whimpered as my heart sped up in my chest.

"I won't hurt you, micah. I'd never cause you any harm. It's always safe, sane, and consensual play. Is that understood?"

i nodded.

He swatted my thigh with His palm. "A verbal response, please."

"Yes, Sir, i understand."

"Good girl," He said, moving about in the playroom.

"Remember My earlier words: you control what happens here. If at any time you wish to stop, we will stop. No questions asked. With that said, let's do a quick refresher. What's your safe word again, micah?"

"my safe word is 'Cookie,' Sir."

"And when do you use your safe word?"

"my safe word is to be used when i want play to stop immediately, Sir. i am to use it when i have reached a physical or emotional breaking point."

"That's My pretty girl. you understand the rules," He replied before my darkness was filled with white light.

my anguished yelp couldn't be helped. The sharpest pain imaginable had just been localized onto my oversensitive nipples.

Fuck!

"Are you fine to proceed, micah?" He asked.

"Y-y-yes, Sir," i managed to stammer out as Rick ran His thumb across my lips.

Cool metal glided across my flesh, momentarily distracting me from the pain in my nipples.

Rick reached between my thighs and once again found my pearl, latching a clamp to it.

The pressure of the clamp's rubber-coated teeth didn't hurt so much as crank up my already heated body to *raging inferno*.

He knew i couldn't do this, couldn't hold back. i was set up like a motherfucker.

That smug look He had given me before sending me into darkness made me want to disobey Him all over again.

Tears slipped from underneath the blindfold, but i refused to use the safe word. i was not a masochist, not by a long shot, but i didn't want to disappoint Him.

Even though i couldn't see Rick, i knew He was watching my every reaction.

He tugged on the chain, which brought the tips of the clamps together, creating a ridiculous amount of pressure. *Shit, that hurt.* i hadn't experienced nipple clamps in a long while. It's an unbearable pain that you never quite forget—that is, if you ever made it through. Kind of what i imagined riding a bike through a minefield might be like.

i was on the cusp of uttering my safe word, but i couldn't let Him break me. Not tonight, not my first time with Him.

"How's My pretty girl doing?" He inquired while stroking my hair.

"i-i-i'm fine, Sir," i replied in between sniffles and gritting my teeth. i tried to think about anything other than my throbbing erogenous zones.

"I'm well aware that you aren't a masochist, micah, and this is probably very uncomfortable for you, but I need you to realize that there are consequences when you disobey Me. Do you understand?"

"Yes, Sir," i replied softly.

While it was still extremely uncomfortable, my body spread-eagle on the Saint Andrew's Cross was His. He was in complete control of my pain and my pleasure. i was getting to know what pleased Him and what His expectations were.

It was important for me to present as a submissive who took her punishment without complaint. Call it a pride thing, but i was never one to back down from a challenge, and i wasn't about to change my track record. Fuck that. But i wanted to please Him above anything else. i was all kinds of conflicted.

i waited for Him to do something, say something. He hadn't touched my body since applying the last clamp. i missed His hands on me. my ears perked up, listening for any clue, when i heard shuffling coming from the direction of the chest of drawers.

i counted backward from one hundred in my head to distract myself from the pain that hung around like a guest who had overstayed their welcome. The pain in my nipples and clit dulled a little, and i was deep in my own headspace when hot droplets dribbled down my nipples and chest.

my screams were quickly cut off by Rick's mouth covering mine. His tongue probed my mouth as His right hand tugged on the clamp attached to my clit. i went to scream again only to have Him swallow my cries. The tears continued to flow unrestrained beneath my blindfold. It took everything in me to suppress my inherent flight-or-flight instincts. i wanted the torture to end, and i had the power to make it all go away, but the desire to surrender fully to Rick was winning. Tonight, i was determined to step outside my usual level of comfort. my stubbornness was all that kept me from crying out my safe word.

He released my mouth to whisper softly in my ear, "you're doing beautifully, micah. I anticipated you using your safe word, but I'm delighted you were able to push yourself. you're very brave, pretty girl."

It took me a moment to realize that the thick liquid that flowed down my chest was hot wax.

Rick never mentioned He was into wax play. Then again, i never asked. It wasn't a topic that we had covered in our lengthy discussions.

As the wax hardened, He took one of my clamped nipples into His mouth, licking and sucking my erect peak. He didn't let the device keep Him from His target.

He released my nipple and whispered in my ear, His breath sending warm sensations down my spine despite the throbbing of my breasts and clit. "micah, you look beautiful at My mercy. you respond pleasingly to My touch. I'm so proud of you. Seeing you in such a vulnerable state is a huge turn-on. you've made My dick incredibly hard."

He wasn't lying. i could feel His erection rub against my belly through the fabric of His slacks. His bare chest pressed close to mine, giving me the skin-to-skin contact that i so desperately craved. His tongue once again invaded my mouth. He kissed me with an agonizing affection, and my body went haywire.

He took His time removing the clamps, His hand lingering near my clit. Rick dragged His finger down my slit, and i flinched at His touch.

i couldn't withstand the sensation; my pearl was so very sensitive.

With a hint of amusement in His tone, He said, "Looks like I wasn't the only one excited by your punishment. you're soaked, micah. your body's reaction tells me you were very turned on by what happened here. And I thought you weren't into pain. It seems like you can tolerate it for a bit and might even find it a little exciting. We've both made a discovery tonight."

At least one of us was amused by the events that had taken place thus far. This body of mine had betrayed me on every level imaginable. *Damn you, body. Damn you and your betrayal.* How i could experience any euphoria in the face of pain was mystifying, but it happened.

i moaned as His digit moved back and forth against my slit. Oh God, the delicious torment. i was flying high.

Despite my clit being sensitive to His touch, i wanted desperately for Him to finger-fuck me again. Rick abruptly ceased teasing my slit and removed my blindfold.

i blinked wildly. It took a minute for my eyes to adjust to the dim lighting and His lust-filled eyes staring into mine. A single tear trickled down my cheek and He wiped it away with His the pad of His thumb.

He worked to release my hands and feet from the restraints and led me away from the Saint Andrew's Cross. i looked down at my tender breasts to find they were covered in red wax. You know something? The color looked great against my deep brown complexion. It may have hurt like a motherfucker, but it looked gorgeous.

After tossing the blindfold and clamps onto the bondage table, Rick used the dimmer to turn off the lights before taking my hand and escorting me down the corridor to His bedroom.

my heels clicked loudly against the hardwood floor with each unsteady step i took.

Once we were inside the bedroom, He fiddled with the dimmer and instructed me to sit on the bed—a luxurious California King covered in a tan and white duvet.

i did as directed while He ducked inside the master bath. i heard water running and Him moving about. A short time later, Rick walked into the bedroom with a basin of soapy water and a washcloth; i couldn't help but notice His erection was still very prominent against the zipper of His slacks. Was His intention to fuck me or at least ask that i pleasure Him with my mouth? We did have that discussion about birth control, but did that mean He was going to use a condom tonight or was He going to wait to fuck me?

i was anxious to see what the bulge He was packing could do. Usually, i'm not one to fuck a guy on the first date, especially since casual sex isn't my cup of tea, but He and i were way past being demure—i was just bound naked to a Cross.

One thing was certain: my mind was brimming with thoughts of writhing beneath Him in ecstasy.

i sat on the edge of the bed with my hands clasped in my lap, still reeling from what had transpired, when He made His way to me. Rick placed the basin on the nightstand before kneeling to remove my heels.

"I wouldn't be a very good Dominant if I didn't take care of you as I should. Please lie down in the middle of the bed," He instructed. The softness in His voice while He tended to my needs was heartwarming.

The clock on the nightstand read 12:47 a.m. It really was true: time *did* fly when you were having fun.

Splayed out in the middle of the bed, i watched Rick plunge the washcloth into the steamy water. A fragrant blend of lavender and rose filled the room.

He wrang out the cloth, then cleaned me from head to toe with an extraordinary amount of tenderness, gently removing all traces of wax from my skin. He spent the most time cleaning my pussy, working in silence and with a delicate touch. The warm water mercifully soothed my extremely sore pearl.

When Rick was done, He stood and returned the basin and washcloth to the bathroom. Moments later, He appeared with a slightly larger damp cloth and hovered over me, quietly wiping my face.

i tried my best to avoid making eye contact but failed miserably. His eyes were hypnotic, and as much as i attempted not to look at Him, my eyes were drawn to His.

He kissed my lips softly before standing to place the cloth on the nightstand. He removed His shoes, socks, and slacks before pulling back the covers, neither of us saying a word.

When He placed His slacks on the armchair, my eyes were again drawn to the bulge in His boxer briefs. Obviously, i was intrigued, but i was also concerned. i last had sex a little over a year ago and it looked like what He was packing would hurt. Dear God, i hoped it hurt so good.

my inner pervert was doing the running man.

The outline of His dick looked thick. i smiled the more i thought about it. Based on our exchange earlier, He wanted exclusivity, and i wanted it too. i had set out to test the waters tonight, but now i wanted to set sail with Rick at the helm.

i licked my lips. i was having a difficult time trying to pull my eyes away from His package. Every time i tried to look away, my eyes went right back to the forbidden destination. It was distracting to say the least, and i think He caught me staring.

i jumped when Rick's voice finally sliced through the silence that lingered between us. "micah, be sure to follow up with your gynecologist this week. Hopefully, you can get an appointment soon. When you receive the prescription, I want you to begin taking it immediately after your next period. It'll be fully effective in about four weeks. Do you have any questions?"

i shook my head feverishly while my eyes traveled down to His beefy thighs. What i wouldn't give to feel my legs wrapped around them.

"Verbalize your response, micah," He replied.

"No, Sir, i don't have any questions. i'll see my doctor, fill the prescription, and start taking the pills after my next cycle."

"Good girl," He said, slipping under the covers and pulling me against Him, His hard-on pressing firmly against my backside.

"How are you feeling? Do you want to talk about what happened back in the playroom? I want you to know that you can tell Me any thoughts you have, negative or positive, about what happened in there. I want you to feel free to express whatever is on your mind, micah."

"i'm okay. At the moment, i don't want to talk, although my brain is going a mile a minute. A lot happened, but if it's fine with You, Sir, i'd like to take some time to process everything.

"But if i want to discuss something specific, i know to bring it to Your attention immediately. Right now, i'd just like to lay here with You."

"We can talk whenever you're ready," He said, pulling me closer to Him. Rick removed an arm from around my waist to reach for the remote on the nightstand.

Before He shut off the lights and the sound system, i turned to face Him. "i do have one question before we call it a night, Sir."

"Go ahead, ask your question."

"Did You want me to relieve Your problem, Sir? my nature is to take care of my Man's needs, and i want to be sure You're satisfied."

"What problem are you referring to, micah?"

i could hear the taunting in His voice. He was trying to make me blush. He wanted me to say it.

"Ah… Your hard-on, Sir. Would You like me to provide You with some, um, relief?" i'm sure He realized how nervous i was asking such a question, but i didn't want to go to sleep without ensuring He was satisfied. It wouldn't hurt that i'd also glimpse what kept poking me in my back and what was now pressed firmly against my belly.

He snuggled against my neck, tightening His grip around my waist. He released a slight chuckle before giving me a quick peck on the lips. "No, pretty girl, not this time. your mouth and your pussy will bring Me a great deal of relief in the future. I'm a very patient Man."

her Master

I awoke the next morning to an empty bed. It was My last day off before I was on rotation for the next few days and micah wasn't here. Fuck.

Pulling the covers back, I climbed out of bed and noticed a note on the nightstand on her side of the bed. *her side of the bed.* A smirk crossed My lips. micah felt so good in My arms last night. she belonged there, and I would do everything to make sure she stayed.

Presently, My dick was angry with Me. My dick was *very* angry with Me. The woman had been so eager to help Me out with My problem. It was hard—no pun intended—falling asleep with her shapely ass rubbing up against Me. I admired her enthusiasm; a Man had to appreciate a lady who loved sucking dick. she would be doing a lot of that in the future, but one thing at a time.

First, I needed to get rid of My morning wood, but before I got down to business, I read micah's note.

Dear Sir,

i didn't want to disturb You, but i needed to leave to get ready for work. i'm under a tight deadline. Because the exhibition is opening in a few weeks, i have a lot to do and calling out today wasn't an option.

i'm sorry i left without saying good-bye, but i didn't want to wake You. Please know that i didn't want to disturb You out of respect. Under any other circumstances, i would never leave without permission. i promise to call You when i have a free moment today. Thank You for last night, it was wonderful. i can't wait to see You again.

XoXo
micah

No smirk this time—this time she got a full smile out of Me. Shit, I couldn't stop smiling. Being with micah made Me, in a word, exultant.

I appreciated her leaving Me a note, but this was My last day off before I'd be on rotation and teaching for the next four days. I wanted to see her.

I tossed the note on the bed and headed to the bathroom. I took a piss, rubbed one out, and got dressed to hit the treadmill in My home gym before I left to go see My girl.

The Whitney Museum. I hadn't been there in years. It was time I made a visit.

Playtime

micah

All afternoon my thoughts were in disarray. What happened last night was, in a word, unbelievable.

Of the Doms i previously served, none compared to Rick. He was intelligent, self-assured, caring, and direct, straddling the line between sensitive and stoic. He turned me on yet terrified me a wee bit. For the first time in a very long time, i'd been forced outside my comfort zone, and i liked it a lot. i hadn't anticipated things going as far as they did last evening, but i had no regrets. my biggest concern right now was how Rick would feel about me departing so abruptly.

He said He wanted to see me again and wanted exclusivity, but you know how Men can be sometimes: They say one thing but mean another.

When a Man like Rick was straightforward and direct, my first inclination was to believe His words, but i'd had the shittiest luck. i wanted to believe His sincerity, but part of me was ever so cautious. Rick was the kind of Guy who seemed too good to be true. Successful, handsome. Basically your tall, dark, and Alpha type.

If someone were to ask, i'd say i was a good judge of character, but sometimes people who initially start off great can completely take you by surprise, and not in a good way.

This morning it took me a moment to recall where i was. Once i got my bearings and my pulse stopped racing, i looked over to where Rick lay. i wanted desperately to give Him my own special version of "good morning." Instead i watched the rhythmic rise and fall of His chest. His face displayed a charming, boyish innocence; i longed to run my fingers through His dark tousled hair.

Each time He exhaled, Rick's lower lip would twitch. It was sexy as hell. i pulled the covers back, hoping to get a look at His elusive package. Sadly He was still clad in His boxer briefs, but He was semi-erect. i took a moment to assess His body. Rick Thomas

72

was a work of art, and i was willing to bet He had the stamina of a bull.

i wanted to reach out and touch Him but thought it best that i didn't. i'm sure He would have woken up and wanted to talk about our evening, since i wasn't ready to discuss much before we fell asleep. i wasn't a booty call, but i wasn't ready to start the day bright-eyed and bushy-tailed discussing what happened last night over a cup of coffee, either.

Don't get me wrong—i loved what i experienced last night, but it scared me *how much* i enjoyed it. It was only our first night together, but i did things i'd never done before. Everything about last night was out of character for me. Connections usually take time to happen; however, on my first date with this Man, i was ready to do whatever He asked.

Morning came too soon. i had to get going or i would be late for work. Slipping from under the covers, i tiptoed out of the bedroom and quietly entered the playroom, grabbing my belongings and dressing. i was sure to leave a note before heading out, but i was confident Rick would be pissed that i left without saying good-bye.

It was probably wrong that i got a little bit of a thrill thinking about that. He was kind of sexy when He was angry.

The day had been filled with firming up last-minute details and making sure all the preparations for the event were handled. In theory, i should have been nervous. This was a high-profile, multimillion-dollar event. The higher-ups made me want to down a bottle of Advil with a vodka chaser, but i wasn't nervous. i was pissed the fuck off.

Today's meeting with Joan and the exhibition manager, Guillaume Chaillot, whom i found to be an eccentric worrywart—the guy had a stick up his ass the size of Texas—nearly turned fatal. He asked Joan twice, while i sat across the table from him, if i was capable of handling the final preparations. That statement alone made me want to blow a gasket. No one should ever, and i do mean ever, question my work ethic or capabilities.

i always get results. i wouldn't be tasked with additional responsibility if i weren't good at my job.

Not once during the meeting did either of them acknowledge the extended hours our staff had been maintaining to make the exhibit as perfect as possible. Joan's and Guillaume's self-absorption was irksome but not surprising, but still, i found it annoying.

The gala would be happening soon, and then i'd resume a life of semi-normalcy.

What would my normal be now that Rick was somewhat in my life?

Before heading to the museum, I met a friend for lunch. Josh and I met about five years ago at a meetup for marathoners. I was prepping for My third New York City Marathon and wanted some new ideas to incorporate into My training. After exchanging info on tempo runs, supplements, and strength-training regimens, We began shooting the shit. Turned out We had a lot more in common than We initially thought.

A few weeks after that meetup, I ran into Josh at an event hosted by a NYC not-for-profit whose goals were to raise awareness of alternative lifestyles and dispel myths about D/s. The not-for-profit group hosted a variety of classes/workshops every Friday evening at a loft space downtown owned by one of the board members. It was a great learning opportunity for those who were interested in specific topics but weren't sure how to obtain the information outside of the World Wide Web. It was low key and everyone who attended wore vanilla attire. It was a fairly relaxing environment. New York City, man—eight-million-plus people, but still a fucking small world. Who would've thought a Guy in My running group would share in My love of D/s and grow to be one of My closest friends?

Josh was also a Dom, but His interests were a bit more extreme than Mine. Being a Sadist, Josh enjoyed shit I got absolutely no thrill from. He was heavily into fisting, golden showers, needle play, and medical play.

The world of kink was vast, and I'd be the last one to knock someone's interests. I saw no problem indulging in fetishes that followed the rules of safe, sane, and consensual play; however, medical fetishism did nothing for Me. Not a thing. Don't even get Me started with pissing and fisting. I could think of many fun things to do with pussy and none of them included sticking My entire hand inside one.

In any case, Our hectic work schedules had made it tough for Josh and I to catch up. Today our free time just happened to overlap, and His law office wasn't too far from My final destination: the Whitney.

When I met Him at the café, Josh immediately started in with twenty questions.

"So who is she?" He asked as We followed the hostess to a corner table.

"Who is what? What are You talking about?" I replied, perusing the lunch specials once We took Our seats.

"Come on. You can't bullshit a Bullshitter, Richard."

I laughed. Now He was hitting below the belt. My mother, My superiors, and a few stick-in-the-mud colleagues were the only people who ever called Me "Richard."

"Oh, it's 'Richard' now, huh?"

Josh rolled His eyes. "Quit stalling. Who's the woman, Rick? And don't even try to deny it; I know something's up."

The waiter set two glasses of water down on Our table before announcing he'd return shortly.

I slowly took a sip of water before responding, "How did You know?"

"You're grinning. You never fucking grin."

See, I told you micah did something to Me. I mean shit, if a Guy who's known Me for quite some time noticed, then she must be having quite an impact.

I paused and took a deep breath before I responded. There was no sense in bullshitting Him.

"Her name is micah. We met a few weeks ago. Well, I initially saw her at Spanxxx but ended up treating her."

"So You're fucking Your patients now?" Josh asked.

I gritted My teeth. This Guy, man, such a douche.

"No, I'm not fucking her, and she's no longer My patient."

"I never thought I'd see the day where Doctor Rick Thomas shat where He ate," Josh replied, laughing.

"Look, it's not what You think. I went to Spanxxx for one of their sub/slave auctions to blow off some steam after a particularly shitty day. Just so happens she had a severe asthma attack at the club. I got the situation under control and ended up treating her at

Kincaid. Thing is, I already had My eye on her before everything happened. I was going to bid on her once the auction got underway."

"Must be a hot little thing. So what's the problem? Other than You not fucking her?"

I couldn't hold in the chuckle that escaped My lips.

"I want to. I want her, *bad*. But . . ."

Josh held up a finger and interrupted Me. "Let Me guess the 'but.' Since samantha did a number on You, You're not sure if You can ever completely trust a woman again." He pursed His lips as if daring Me to challenge His assessment. "And We're not talking just any woman, but a woman You want to take as Your sub. Are My Spidey senses on target?"

"Something like that," I replied.

"No, it's exactly that. Don't downplay what's going on, I know You, Bro. I'm not going to tell You what to do. I'm sure I'll find out details about her if and when the time is right, but whatever You do, don't be that Guy. Don't pursue her if You can't get Your shit together."

He leaned forward and gave Me a pointed look. "Don't lead her on. You hated when sam did it to You, so don't do it to this girl."

I turned My attention to the salt and pepper shakers on the table as a distraction, and lightly tapped the top of the pepper. The dreaded sam. He had a point. I was still a little gun-shy but I definitely wasn't leading micah on.

I leaned back in the chair, crossing My arms over My chest. "Last night was the first time I let go in a long time. I laid it on the line. You of all people know I don't do vulnerable, but last night I gave in. I opened up and let go. she was in My playroom, Josh. My fucking playroom."

My throat suddenly felt dry. I took another swig of water. "You know I don't bring anyone there. The experience was surreal and I felt drawn to her, that's the scariest part. We're still in the early stages, but I'm so incredibly taken with her."

I paused for a moment, letting Josh take in what I'd just revealed before continuing, "she spent the night."

Josh whistled. "Well, well, well. You had a woman over to Your place? You like her? she stayed overnight? And You didn't fuck her? Am I following this okay?"

"Yeah. That's an accurate summation."

"Hmm, before You go letting Your heart into the game, why not have a little sexy time with her first? Test the waters before You commit. she could be a dud in the sack for all You know, and that would be tragic, My Friend."

"Josh, You're a pig," I replied. "Pussy isn't everything. Did You know there's more to a woman than what's between her legs?"

"There is? Who knew? I may be a pig, but I'm a pig who knows to test the waters before heavily investing in anything. Always test-drive the product."

I shook My head. There was never a dull moment with Josh. I had no further desire to discuss micah. Josh was cool, but He didn't get it. He may never get it.

I was thankful when He abruptly changed the subject.

He leaned forward again, hunching over the table. "Man, have I got a story for You. Met this chick the other night and had a fantastic time. Tight little body with out-of-this-world tits, and she gives the best head I've ever had."

I shook My head again. Sometimes Josh had the mentality of a horny eighteen-year-old getting laid for the first time.

"Totally submissive, and I think she may even be a bit of a masochist."

I laughed. "You're getting Your dick sucked by some random broad? Did You forget You're sharing Your unsafe sexual practices with a Doctor? For a Lawyer, a smart one at that, You indulge in some risky shit, Josh. A Guy in His forties should know better."

"Screw You. It was invite-only so everyone was already pre-screened. It's not like I was messing around with a hooker. It was a group of about fifty of us at Mistress Carlisle's place. You know She throws some insane bashes."

"What's her name? Do You even know?" I asked.

Josh's eyes darted around the café before focusing His attention on the menu.

I laughed out loud. "You don't even know her name. Priceless."

"I think it was lisa. Shit, I don't know, but I hope I run into her again, that's for sure. The woman had skills. I'm telling You, best of My life."

I smirked as the waiter returned to take Our order. Josh and I continued to chat until Our food arrived. Since neither of Us had much more time to spare, We ate quickly and agreed to plan a run in the coming weeks before parting ways.

Before I left the café, I picked up some lunch for micah. Armed with a ham-and-cheese croissant, an apple, and a bottle of water, I swung by the florist and purchased a dozen Belle Rouge roses for My pretty girl. I could have chosen any flower, but when I saw the rich red petals, I thought of micah's lips.

Goddamn, I wondered how her lips would look wrapped around My dick.

If I kept up this line of thinking, I'd need a cold shower and would never make it to the Whitney.

With My arms full, I stood at the museum's security desk, locked in a battle of wits with one of the guards, and somehow the motherfucker was winning. I was trying My best to remain calm and dignified, and not use crass language, but the guard was irritating Me with his belittling demeanor.

I had been flying high thinking of My time with micah and how I'd see her shortly. I didn't need some asshole raining on My parade.

I eyed the elevators behind the security desk, which I assumed led to the offices of the museum personnel. My patience was wearing thin since one guard in particular kept repeating, "Personnel aren't allowed visitors."

I tried to reason with him and explain I wasn't "visiting" but there to drop off a gift for My girl. In a way, I was glad the guy was serious about his job; it meant micah's best interests were at the forefront. But I wanted to see her, and he was preventing that from happening.

After her abrupt departure, I wanted to know she was okay.

I could honestly say I smiled more in the past twenty-four hours than I had in the past month. I hadn't meshed with a woman in a very long time and I enjoyed this new feeling. I probably had a silly, lopsided grin plastered on My face. Of course Josh had noticed.

Well, My smile quickly turned into a scowl when the guard waved his hand in front of My face, attempting to gain My attention.

"What part of 'Ms. Foster isn't allowed visitors' don't you understand?" he inquired.

It was becoming increasingly difficult to keep My temper in check. This guy was really testing Me. My voice had already gotten louder, causing people to stop and stare. The last thing I wanted to do was make a spectacle of Myself. I took a few deep breaths before responding to the condescending jab.

"For the third time, I am not a visitor. I want to drop some things off for her. Calling Me a visitor would imply I'm staying. I'll be leaving as soon as I give her these things. Can you simply call her and tell her that her . . ."

Wait, what was I? I couldn't very well tell this asshole that I was a Dom and micah was under My tutelage. So I thought of the next best thing, something he'd understand.

"Tell ms. foster that Rick is here to see her."

"And just who are you to Ms. Foster, Rick?"

Who am I? Yeah, I knew he'd ask. The asshole seemed a little defensive in his inquisition. Was this part of his job or was he busting My balls because he had a crush on My pretty girl?

Sorry, guy, your world is about to come crumbling the fuck down.

Since My hands were full, I couldn't get in His face like I wanted to, so I leaned across the security desk far enough for there to be no mistaking the intent behind My words. "I'm her Boyfriend."

The guard's face deflated. Reluctantly, he leaned over his partner's shoulder and picked up the phone on the desk.

"I'll call her now."

A victorious grin curled My lips. My stake had been claimed.

"Thank you very much," I said, displaying My biggest and brightest smile. Normally, I'm not the jealous type—I'm secure in My shit—but when you try to assert power you don't have just to bust My balls because you're lusting after someone who doesn't even know you exist, then you just made it to number one on My shit list. In My line of work, I deal with all types, but to deal with an antagonistic personality in this instance? No way, not happening.

"Yes. Hi, Ms. Foster? It's Jim from security. We have someone here named Rick claiming to be your boyfriend at the desk near the L-17 entrance. He has some things to give you. If you could come downstairs as soon as possible, I'd appreciate it."

Claiming? Better tread lightly, Jim. I leaned against the desk, taking in My surroundings. Glad that shit was nipped in the bud. micah appeared a few moments later, sauntering toward Me and looking striking in an orange tank that emphasized her mouthwatering cleavage and a blue pencil skirt that hugged her hips.

she was runway perfect, at least in My eyes. Maybe Jim's, too. He was looking a little too hard at My girl, and as much as I wanted to show him who he was dealing with, I had to reel it in for micah's sake. No sense in making a scene at her place of employment.

As she made her approach, I took the opportunity to assess her from toe to head. The strappy sandals she wore matched the color of her skirt. The heels defined her shapely calves even more.

Everything about micah was sexy.

Last night her hair was in soft waves; today it was styled in some sort of curly afro. I loved it. she was perfect.

micah's face was impassive as she made her way toward the security desk.

I knew My visit was spontaneous, and she was likely very busy, but I had to see her.

Was she glad to see Me? Leaving a note was considerate, but I would have much preferred she had woken Me up before leaving. she left while I was sleeping, and that nagged at Me.

My question was answered when she arrived at the security desk wearing a megawatt smile.

Happily, I bent down to greet her with a kiss on the lips. It was a struggle not to drop everything and wrap My arms around her curvy little body. Those lips of hers were so damn tasty, I could suck on them all day.

"Hi, micah."

For a brief moment, her face flashed alarm and she hesitated in her response.

We hadn't yet established proper public protocol. I'm sure she was concerned about how to address Me. Of course, the nosy guard watched our every move. I gave a slight nod before clearing My throat.

"Hi, Honey," she replied with a smile and a wink.

A sly smile graced My lips. *Atta girl.*

"I come bearing gifts. I missed you this morning. you left without saying good-bye."

"Thank You," she replied, accepting My offerings.

I leaned forward to whisper in her ear, "I was hoping to wake up to your delectable naked form, but you took that opportunity away from Me. Tsk, tsk."

she looked flustered. "i-i had to make sure i made it to work on time. i'm sorry. i was sure to leave a note."

"I know, I saw. Much appreciated."

As she sniffed the bouquet, I gently grabbed her elbow and led her away from the guard's prying ears.

Now that My hands were free, I relished in touching her. Bending, I kissed her again, My lips lingering against hers before moving to her neck. "Nice save, sweetheart," I said, inhaling deeply just behind her ear.

My God, did she make My mouth water.

"i'm sorry if i was out of line, but i knew i couldn't call you 'Sir' without raising a few brows." With the vase of roses tucked tightly against her hip, she stepped away from Me, leaning against the wall as she raised her eyebrow. "We haven't established how You prefer to be addressed, so i just went with what came to mind."

I waved off her comment. "It's fine. I appreciate the quick thinking."

she dropped her gaze and shifted where she stood.

"you know, micah," I said, taking a step toward her and raising her chin so she could meet My eyes, "we still have a lot to talk about."

her eyelids fluttered before she blinked slowly. her long lashes curled in a way that called to Me, drawing Me in closer and closer.

I rested My hand against her cheek. So soft. So warm. So beautiful . . .

"Sir?" she whispered.

I swallowed and blinked, remembering why I was there. It was so easy to get lost in those wide, dark brown eyes of hers.

"Like I said, I would've preferred to wake up to you naked beside Me. I hope you not disturbing Me wasn't due to any embarrassment."

she gave me what appeared to be a shy smile. "You're welcome, Sir," she replied, hesitating a moment before continuing, "i enjoyed last night."

I think if micah had been of a lighter hue, she'd be blushing.

"It was early when i woke, and i thought it be best that i slip out quietly. my intention was to give You a call during my lunch hour."

Hmm, she didn't address being embarrassed. Interesting. "Well, there's no need for a call now." I brushed a stray curl off her face. "Next time, be sure to wake Me."

"Of course, Sir."

"We can discuss how to address Me in public in greater detail later, but when we're among business associates, vanilla friends, or family, Rick is fine."

I wanted her to meet every damn person I knew. I'd take great pride having micah on My arm. "Sweetheart, Honey, Baby, and whatever charming nicety you want to use is also acceptable. When we're in private, amongst like-minded individuals, or when we play, it's Sir, unless different rules have been agreed upon. Is that understood?"

she nodded.

"Verbalize your response, please," I replied with a pointed look. she'd have to work on that.

"Yes, Sir, i understand."

I glanced over to the security desk to see the guard frowning at Me and micah. Fuck that guy.

"So how long has that asshole had his sights on you?" I asked, nodding toward the guard.

she let out a hearty laugh, and My dick jerked in My jeans. Really? Was there anything about her that wouldn't turn Me on?

"He's harmless, Sir, but he's asked me out for coffee a few times. i've always declined his offers. i think You being here and identifying Yourself as my Boyfriend pretty much put the brakes on him asking me again, so thank You."

"No need to thank Me. To outsiders, I am your Boyfriend, micah, but we both know I'm more than that. Remember what I said about exclusivity?"

she looked down at her bouquet and flicked a petal with her thumb. "Well, we never had a formal conversation about it, Sir. i wasn't sure what to make of Your statement."

"Well, it's not the best location, but we're having a formal conversation now. How's this for clarity? I want you, and only you. What uncertainty do you have, micah? I don't cheat and I don't share."

she looked up at My face momentarily before fiddling with the rose petals. her attention then shifted to the guards' station. "i should really get back upstairs. There's lots of work to be done," she replied.

she was running away.

Sure, I had My own issues, but I was trying. I needed her to do the same.

"micah, if you have reservations, talk to Me, but don't pull away, please. I'm trying here, but it goes both ways. I'd love for us to continue moving forward. I would like to see you again tonight since I'm back on rotation for the rest of the week. Seeing each other might be impossible then."

she ceased toying with the petals and met My gaze. she did that lip-biting thing I'd grown accustomed to.

"So what do you say? Will you please stay with Me tonight?"

"i'm not sure what time i'll get out of here. i've been in meetings all day, and with the opening happening soon, i might not leave until after eight. Before i could even think about heading to Your place, Sir, i'd have to eat, shower, and pack a bag. The timing is iffy."

micah probably had a rejection handy for every situation.

"Here's what I need you to do for Me. After work, go home and get your things. I'll take care of the rest."

Moments passed and she still hadn't given Me an answer. Fucking frustrating.

"micah? Stop thinking so hard. I'm pretty sure you're out of excuses."

Silence.

"micah?" I probed.

she sighed. "Okay. i'll call You when i'm on my way, Sir."

Why the sigh? I was honestly confused. she seemed excited to see Me and said she enjoyed last night. Women—so goddamn frustrating.

"Please take a cab, I don't want you on the subway at such a late hour. Once you call Me and let Me know you're on your way, I'll wait in the lobby and take care of the fare."

I bent down to give her a kiss good-bye. I couldn't help imagining My face between her thighs. This woman did all kinds of shit to My head—the big one and the not-so-little one.

"I'll see you tonight," I whispered in her ear.

she licked her lips.

That lone gesture made Me want to push her up against a wall and fuck her silly. I had plans for micah, but I needed to keep the head above My shoulders in the game and not let the head below My waist cloud My judgment.

Cupid was taunting Me.

Was this love at first sight? I didn't know. Lust was certainly prevalent.

I could fall for her—I was falling for her. Moving at micah's pace was going to be agony, pure agony.

she gave Me one last peck on the lips.

"Thank You again for lunch and the flowers. i'll see You tonight, Honey," she said loud enough for the guard to hear before turning on her heel and heading to the elevators. she glanced back to give Me a wink before disappearing from My view.

The silly grin micah inspired turned into a taunting smirk when My gaze shifted to the security desk. Jim stood there staring daggers at Me.

micah

i was still reeling from Rick's surprise appearance. i can't believe He took time out of His day to bring me lunch and flowers. Inwardly, i was squealing like a teenage girl.

Rick didn't just bring any flowers, He brought the most beautiful red roses i had ever had the pleasure of receiving. His impeccable taste didn't truly surprise me; His clothing and His home were aesthetic and now i could add His choice of florists to the growing list.

i wasn't sure what to make of His request to see Me tonight. i was excited but still reserved. Hell, i was still processing all that happened.

i had called kisa early this morning, while i was in a cab en route to my apartment after leaving Rick's. First i had to let her know that i was okay because i didn't check in last night, and then i wanted to share all the details of my amazing night.

kisa hung on my every word but not before reprimanding me for not calling her sooner. i apologized profusely. It had never been my intention to worry her, but knowing kisa, she would never let me live that down.

While i sat in my office eating the lunch Rick brought me, i recalled kisa's words.

"micah, i'm really happy for you. Things sound like they went really well last night, but i wouldn't be a good friend if i didn't tell you to be careful."

"Careful? He wouldn't hurt Me, kisa. i don't get that vibe from Him."

"i wasn't referring to physical harm. It sounds like you're getting emotionally attached to this Guy. Don't go too fast too soon, micah. i know you're a die-hard romantic, but take it easy, chica."

Was she serious?

she fucked Doms every which way from Sunday trying to find her glass dick, but she was telling me to slow down? Cinderella had nothing on kisa. The fairy-tale princess was an amateur.

i loved the woman like a sister, but she should have given me some credit. i wasn't some glassy-eyed ditz.

While i valued kisa's opinion, i was offended that she would think i wasn't using good judgment. What happened last night wasn't the norm for me. It wasn't something that i did, ever. i may scene with Men at clubs, but it doesn't get this personal. It's *never* this personal. kisa was well aware of how out of character this was for me. i have a hard and fast rule: Never get emotionally invested. But it was clear from the way things were going with Rick that that rule had changed.

"kisa, when have you ever known me to spend the night with a Man i barely know, allow Him to tie me up, blindfold me, eat me out, and then spoon me and treat me as if i were the most precious gem on the face of the earth? Hmm?"

kisa huffed and attempted to get in a rebuttal but i cut her off before she had the chance. "Would 'never' be an accurate response?" i asked.

i paused and took a deep breath. i was upset that she would think so little of me.

"micah, calm down. Don't get upset. i'm just trying to provide some perspective. i hope this is it, i really do, but guard your heart. If He's true, He will work for you. He will want to earn you. Don't invest too much in Him until He proves Himself worthy. And if you're not ready for this, leave now before you're in too deep."

kisa may have her priorities screwed but she was right. If Rick was serious about me, He would do whatever possible to make it work between us. i just had to be smart about it and let His actions speak for themselves. So far, He was doing well. Really, really, really well.

i had to stop pulling back. He was trying, and i couldn't keep sending mixed messages. i wanted something real, and if Rick was the One to give it to me, i had to let Him in and not be afraid to let go.

But was He it for me?

It was approaching 10:45 p.m. and i was exhausted. Going over the mountain of paperwork Joan dropped off earlier had kept me in the office until a little after nine. i had to be escorted out of the museum by an armed guard. Rarely had i ever worked that late, but when Cruella beckoned before an opening, you listened. Two of my staffers also stayed late to make the process go that much faster. Bless their little hearts.

The distance from my place to Rick's wasn't far, and with the late hour, you'd think the cab would practically fly there. But New York is the city that never sleeps; there was always something popping off. The crosstown drive should have taken fifteen minutes, tops. Tonight it took twice as long.

Time and my overactive mind were not good company. When the cab finally pulled up to Rick's building, my nerves almost had me begging the cabbie to turn around.

Before i could open my mouth, a kindly looking middle-aged man opened the cab door and welcomed me to the building. The man barely finished his sentence before the smooth bass of the Man that had been in my head all day interrupted him.

"I'll take it from here, Paul." Rick's smiling face filled my vision and i forgot my own name. He reached in and handed the driver a twenty. "Keep the change."

i gathered my purse and overnight bag before Rick took my hand and helped me from the cab.

"Doctor Thomas, would you like me to bring your guest's bag to the elevator?" the door attendant asked.

"No, that won't be necessary, Paul. By the way, this is micah, micah foster, My girlfriend. You'll be seeing her around a lot more."

Paul raised a curious brow, and my stomach chose that exact moment to do a mini somersault.

From the look on Paul's face i could tell Rick didn't use the title of "girlfriend" often. He also mentioned that He didn't bring women to His playroom, so i assumed that meant His apartment in general. This was big. i felt pretty damn special.

"It's a pleasure to meet you, Micah," the door attendant said, extending his hand.

i reached out to shake it. "Nice to meet you as well, Paul."

"You two have a good night," Paul said before we made our way through the lobby.

"And you as well," Rick replied while taking my overnight bag in one hand and placing the other on the small of my back. Once we reached the elevators, He removed His hand from my back and pressed the button. Almost immediately, one set of elevator doors sprung open. He allowed me to enter first, following closely behind.

As soon as the doors closed, He was all over me.

Rick delivered a trail of feather-light kisses along my jawline and neck. His kisses continued, each one more needy than the last. my nipples perked up. He soon changed His path, and His lips forcefully met mine.

i welcomed the invasion. What we were doing was on the verge of illicit, but i hadn't a care in the world.

Rick slowly pulled away from my lips. "Hi," He whispered, nibbling my top lip. His hardened frame felt wonderful against me. "I've been thinking about you since I left the museum."

He had obliterated my personal space. i didn't mind, not one bit, especially since He smelled so damn good, like the outdoors. His scent evoked memories of apple-picking, pumpkin farms, and hiking. i loved it. It made me feel safe. i leaned into Him further, inhaling deeply.

"Hi, Sir," i replied, barely able to catch my breath.

Before i could get another word out, His tongue once again probed my mouth. We stood inside the elevator kissing for what felt like an eternity before Rick finally released me and pushed the button for the twenty-fifth floor.

He rested His back against the elevator panel and pulled a handkerchief from His back pocket. Wiping His mouth, He rid Himself of my lipstick. "I apologize if I was a bit aggressive. I was anxious to see you."

i licked my lips, suddenly so very thirsty under Rick's heavy stare. i cleared my throat. "There's nothing wrong with that, Sir. It feels good to be wanted."

"micah, you have no idea how badly I want you."

i wasn't certain how to respond, so i remained quiet.

Rick released a slight chuckle before placing the handkerchief back into His pocket.

"Do I make you uncomfortable, micah? I get the impression I do. When I express My desires, you do this thing where you withdraw and head into your own world. Might I ask what that's about?"

Was He really trying to get into my head right now, when there was so much less risk involved with getting into my pants?

"i . . . uh . . . i think sometimes i'm just a little overwhelmed."

"Hmm, I certainly don't want you to feel overwhelmed. If you ever need a moment, it's important for you communicate that to Me."

"Yes, Sir, i understand."

The elevator stopped on His floor and the doors parted. Rick waited for me to exit first before walking ahead of me down the hallway. He paused, opening the door to His apartment, gesturing for me to enter.

"You left Your door unlocked, Sir?" i asked, turning to give Him a quizzical look as i stepped across the threshold.

Clearly, He was amused by my concern. "I live in a secure building, sweetheart. A quick trip downstairs to fetch you isn't cause for concern. I get that it's New York City, but I think we're safe here. The fees I pay on this place say the safety of the tenants is a top priority," He said while locking the door.

"Oh. i guess i'm overly cautious."

"And that isn't a bad thing. I'd rather you were overly cautious than not." His voice trailed down the corridor as He made His way to the bedroom with my bag in tow.

i stood near the door, holding my purse and waiting for His return.

"Make yourself at home, micah. Head to the kitchen, I'll be right there to make you something to eat. I'm sure you're famished," He yelled from the bedroom.

He was right: i was hungry. i hadn't eaten much since the lunch He provided for me earlier in the day.

i removed my jacket and dropped it, along with my purse, on the couch before heading into the kitchen. Sitting on the granite countertop were a variety of takeout containers and a bottle of Merlot. i leaned against the counter, reading the label on the evening's wine selection.

Rick entered the kitchen and removed two plates from the cabinet. i excused myself to wash my hands, returning moments later to see Him withdrawing utensils from the drawers.

"I hope you like Thai. It's mostly vegetable combinations and rice noodles with different sauces. There's also a side of brown rice. I didn't think you'd want anything too heavy this late in the evening."

"Thank You, Sir. i love Thai. And veggies with noodles is fine."

He began filling both our plates while i went to take seat at the kitchen table.

"Wait a moment, micah," He said before pulling the chair away from the table and waiting for me to sit down. Such a Gentleman.

"Thank You," i replied just before He pushed my seat closer to the table.

He smiled before returning to the counter to uncork the wine. Rick brought our food to the table and poured us both glasses of wine before finally settling into the seat across from me.

i dove into the curried mixture as if it were my last meal. i hadn't realized how hungry i was until that moment.

He chuckled at how quickly i ate my portion. "Guess you were hungry, huh?"

"i'm sorry, i don't usually pig out like that," i replied before taking a few sips of wine.

"It's fine. you've had a long day. Would you like more? There's plenty."

"No, thank You, Sir. This was good enough. i'll just finish my wine."

i sat watching Him eat until He finally broke the silence. "Did you happen to follow up with your gynecologist today, micah?"

"Yes, Sir, i did. No appointment necessary. She was able to call in a new prescription to my local pharmacy, but i won't be able to take the pills until next week, since my cycle begins later this week."

"Good to know. What day do you expect it to start?"

"Around Wednesday, the twenty-fourth, Sir."

"I'm keeping a mental note. And does your cycle usually last five days?" He inquired.

"Yes, Sir, it does."

It was a good thing i'd already finished eating. The way i grew up, we didn't talk about private functions at the dinner table. my brother and i were removed from family meals for dirty jokes and whatnot more times than either of us could count.

"I want you to know I take your hard limits very seriously, micah, so there will be no play or anything of a sexual nature while you're menstruating. I want you to be comfortable when we're together."

Boy, was i thankful for that. During my period all i wanted to do was pull up my granny panties, then curl up into fetal position while eating chocolate and watching horrible B-movies on Netflix. So incredibly unsexy.

"Thank You, Sir, i appreciate that."

i sipped my wine, silently watching Rick eat. i was content in the silence. Once He was done, He stood to clear the plates from the table.

"If you're finished with your wine, micah, please go relax for a bit. If you want to shower, I've placed your bag in the master bath. I'll join you in the bedroom shortly."

i took one last sip of my wine and stood from the table. "Yes, Sir."

she looked tired, but that didn't take away from her beauty.

It was late. I imagine micah was exhausted since she hadn't slept much the previous night and then was up early. micah could have messy hair and bags under her eyes, but I would still find her attractive.

Planning for the museum exhibition's opening night had to be draining her, and as much as I didn't want to keep her up late, this would be the last bit of quality time I would get to spend with her for a few days.

I needed to figure out how to best integrate micah into My life. With My work schedule being so jam-packed, it had always been difficult to maintain a steady relationship. Since samantha, there hadn't been a woman in My life whom I wanted to spend a significant amount of time with. Now I needed to rethink My schedule if micah and I were going to make it.

Shit, just to have lunch with Josh was a feat. With micah, interactions a few times a week could break us, especially in the beginning stages. A D/s relationship required time to build, and if You weren't present enough for Your submissive, why bother? It would be unfair to both parties involved.

I put the leftover takeout in the fridge and straightened up the kitchen before heading to the bedroom. I heard the shower running and went to work on spoiling My pretty girl.

Once I had stripped down to My boxer briefs, I gathered a bunch of candles from the hall closet and strategically placed them around the bedroom. After the storm we endured a few weeks ago, I had stocked up on supplies at Home Depot; it's always good to be prepared.

Tonight, the candles would aid in complete relaxation.

Before lighting the candles, I turned on the sound system. Sade crooned about a special someone in her life overtaking her like a quiet storm.

How right she was.

I was trying hard to win micah's heart. she trusted Me enough to come to My home, but as far as I knew, her heart wasn't in the equation. Never in My life had I wanted anyone so badly, and it was a battle to rein in My lust.

I didn't exactly have a fully planned-out seduction; My intention was to let micah know how good I could be to her. How good I could be *for* her.

I returned to the hall closet to grab a few extra-large fluffy towels. Back in the bedroom, I turned the comforter down and spread the towels out across the bed. Once the lights were dimmed, I took My place in the armchair in the corner and waited.

A minute or two later, micah appeared in the doorway with a towel wrapped tightly around her body. The steam from the shower seeped into the bedroom, filling it with the essence of her. Seeing her in an aura of soft light and steam felt as if a vise had attached itself to My heart. she was mesmeric.

she jumped, apparently startled to see Me sitting in the armchair. her curly afro no longer framed her face; it was neatly tamed and held in place by some sort of headband. her face was also bare. Although micah didn't wear much makeup, it was a treat to see her fresh-faced. she looked much younger than her thirty years.

"I'm sorry I startled you. Are you finished?" I inquired as My fingertips grazed the armrest of the chair. I had to do something with My hands to stop Myself from touching her.

she dropped her gaze to the floor before responding, "Yes, Sir. May i get dressed?"

"No, I don't want you dressed. I'd like you to remove your towel and lay across the ones I've placed on the bed."

she followed My instructions without hesitation, slowly removing the bath towel from around her body and placing it on the bed before climbing up and laying on her stomach.

While she got comfortable, I rose from the armchair and headed into the bathroom to find a basket that contained a variety of massage oils. I sifted through the basket, choosing the bottle of coconut and hibiscus oil. Sweet and tangy, just like micah. I brought the bottle back to the bedroom and stared at micah's glorious nude form laying across My bed.

her ass was a goddamn masterpiece, so round and full. I never considered Myself to be an ass Man, but micah made Me rethink a lot of shit.

she gave Me liberties I was certain she hadn't given many Men. We were only at the beginning of our relationship, but she had placed a great deal of trust in Me. micah was stepping outside of her comfort zone and probably trusted Me more than previous partners, and that made My heart swell. Considering we just met, that was a big fucking deal. I was honored by her gesture and wanted to show her that putting her faith in Me was a good decision.

With her eyes closed, she folded her arms under her chin and waited patiently for My next move.

I inched onto the bed. While straddling micah's buttocks, I opened the bottle of oil and drizzled a modest amount down her spine. she flinched when the oil made contact with her skin. I don't think she was anticipating a massage.

"I figured you needed to relax," I said as My hands traveled over her shoulder blades and arms, rubbing the oil into her skin, the deep brown color glistening under My fingertips.

"Mmm. Thank you, Sir. This feels really good," she replied with a low, throaty moan.

Fuck. Although My intentions were good, this was clearly going to be a test of will. I wanted nothing more than to turn her over and bury Myself deep inside her pussy. Being in her presence gave Me some next-level blue balls.

God, I wanted her, but she wasn't someone I just wanted to fuck.

"Glad you're enjoying yourself, sweetheart," I managed to croak out, hoping she hadn't noticed the increased pitch in My voice.

Thirty-seven years old and a woman I hadn't even fucked yet was figuratively bringing *Me* to My knees. Isn't it ironic how the tables can turn?

Thing is, many people have misconceptions about D/s and what it entails. Some misunderstood, thinking it meant having to detach Your feelings and not admit to any vulnerabilities, that somehow because You led, You were incapable of loving and being loved.

Of course, there were the types who believed that for a Man to be considered a Dom, He had to bark orders and belittle a woman in order to be taken seriously and gain her respect. Being a menacing asshole didn't make you a Dom, it just made you an asshole, plain and simple.

Needless to say, a lot of people had it all wrong.

Ultimately, D/s was about tapping into inherent personality traits and finding someone who truly understood them. The yin to Your yang.

A submissive demeanor, to Me, didn't mean "less than."

Personally, I've never had an interest in a woman I could walk all over. Never been attracted to the doormat type, and frankly, I don't get how that's appealing, but to each Their own. I wanted My woman strong-willed, smart, funny, and assertive in her everyday life. she would give most people a run for their money, but when we were together, she would bend to no one's will but Mine.

Outside of our dynamic, she'd be kicking ass and taking names, but when it was the two of us, she would willingly relinquish control.

her duty would be to serve Me, but service would be a two-way street. You had to give in order to get. A submissive would give You her trust, her loyalty, and her vulnerabilities all on a silver platter.

Submissiveness was often referred to as "a gift." Truer words had never been spoken. One shouldn't accept such a gift unless One was fully prepared for all the intricacies a D/s dynamic entailed.

I couldn't imagine My life without kink. I'm simply not made for a vanilla lifestyle. Besides, a little bondage could do wonders for One's sex life. I would describe tying My partner up and fucking her senseless with her legs hoisted up over My arms, her hands bound while I delivered unforgiving thrusts to her slick channel, as heavenly. Shit, it didn't get any better than that.

Before micah, I think the reason why I remained single was due to incompatibility. The toughest part for Me had always been dating. My dating difficulties weren't due to My inability to attract women.

It had never been easy to let them know where My interests lay. I stopped trying to convert vanilla women long ago. It was better to pursue women who knew who they were and wanted the type of relationship I was seeking. I hadn't met a worthwhile match until now.

I've been known to be direct, but with micah I wanted to say a lot more than I had. Timing was everything.

I proceeded to knead her buttocks before pouring more oil into My hands. Since she was in an unguarded state, I couldn't think of a better time to ask My questions.

"Since you're in such a relaxed state, micah, let's talk."

I must have been doing something right because she could barely answer Me through all the moaning she was doing. I finally heard her soft voice respond, "Yes, Sir. What would You like to talk about?"

I pressed My hands against her trapezii and moved down and out to her arms. There was nowhere for her to hide, but she could still lock herself up inside her head. I had to tread lightly. If micah became too worked up, her asthma could be triggered. It seemed to be under control, but I didn't want to chance it.

"sweetheart," I said, continuing the circuit up and down her arms, then down and up her spine.

she hummed a reply but then corrected herself. "Yes, Sir?" she said in a barely-there voice.

"I'm very fond of you . . . probably too fond of you. We've already discussed a lot of what we sought in a partner, but what else is it you need out of this type of dynamic?"

micah took a deep breath but didn't say anything.

I kept talking as I rubbed oil over her body. "Things are progressing quickly, so I wanted to know if you were interested in signing a contract and collaring. But . . ." I paused to gauge her reaction. There was none, except that her body was now rigid beneath Me. Shit. "But first I need to know why you pull away and sink within yourself."

I continued to try and loosen her stiff muscles. Sighing, I kept going. "I've been up-front with you. What you see is what you get with Me. I can be what you need, micah, if you just let Me."

her silence was pushing Me to the end of My patience. "Look. you're not the only one who's been hurt. If this is too much, if you don't want to take a chance with Me, let Me know now. I don't want to waste time on a dead end."

The music lulled and the room became quiet as My hands traveled down her body, rubbing oil onto the backs of her thighs. The candles flickered while I awaited her response.

The silence was unbearable.

"micah?"

"Yes."

"Yes what?"

I shifted as she turned to lay on her back. When My eyes met hers, micah looked as if she were on the verge of tears. I sat atop her legs waiting for her to speak, all while My heart pounded in My chest.

It suddenly dawned on Me that this may not be what she wanted.

What if she said she wanted to walk away?

I didn't fully grasp the consequences of her leaving. I didn't want her to go, and I wasn't prepared to hear her say she was done.

"i'm scared," she whispered.

My heart was beating erratically. *she can't say no. I can't let her say no.* As much as I dreaded what might come out of her mouth next, I had to hear it.

"What are you scared of, micah? Talk to Me."

she licked her lips and wiped her eyes before speaking.

Shit, there were tears. Tears when I asked a serious question wasn't a good sign, but I let her speak.

"When i picture my ideal relationship, it's always with someone i can be myself with. No gimmicks, no false pretenses, no holding back. For so long i've wanted to be cherished and adored by a Man who understood me. i've want to be with a Man who is secure in who He is and what He desires. i've always wanted to be with a Man who would know how to balance kink with everyday life."

she paused, not meeting My eyes, as if there was so much more to unload. I steeled Myself waiting for the worst.

Despite her tears, her voice increased in strength.

"After so many failed attempts, You're doing and saying all the right things, Sir, and i guess i'm just waiting for the other shoe to drop. i just don't believe it's that easy. It's never this easy. When things are too good to be true, they often are."

she gave Me a look that begged Me not to be full of shit. I get the skepticism; I felt the same way. I didn't want her to tell Me all of this just to say good-bye.

micah attempted to wriggle from underneath Me and sit up. she finally gave up when she realized I wouldn't relent and release her. "You keep thinking i'm going to change my mind and walk out of this. i keep thinking You're going to shatter my heart into a million pieces. Ideally, i'd like to be collared. i would hope that my collaring would lead to marriage and starting a family."

she wanted the same thing I did. Forever.

"i believe there's a way to balance it all, Sir. The two people involved have to want it bad enough."

she lay there beneath Me with her eyes and heart wide open. she was so small and so brave.

I heard her. Heard her asking Me for what she needed. And here I was, ready to provide.

Resting My hands on either side of her face, I leaned forward so we were nearly nose to nose. "All you have to do is let Me in."

she skimmed her hand up My arm and then hooked My neck. micah closed the distance between us, pressing her breasts against My bare chest and her lips against Mine.

A deep moan caught in My throat when micah's mouth became more insistent. she held Me tighter, taking My lower lip between her teeth, nipping and suckling, and driving Me out of My mind. micah's hands were everywhere, clawing and groping My flesh. she was wild and her rebellion lit a fire within Me.

I pushed her legs apart and slid My hand between us. Moaning into My mouth, micah spread her legs even wider. The heat radiating from micah's sex had My dick weeping for mercy, for relief. All I had to do was pull down My waistband and slip inside her.

My release was so close.

But I couldn't. I wouldn't do it.

What I felt for her was way past lust and infatuation. I had just asked the woman writhing beneath Me to put her trust in Me, but I was holding back.

For the past few years, I'd been selfish and used women for nothing more than My sexual pleasure. I had detached My emotions from the act, but now I wanted to feel. I wanted to let the connection flourish. I was already in deep when it came to micah. My actions reflected My intent but I needed to be able to say three words that would show her My heart.

My fingers' quick pace brought a look of utter pleasure to micah's face as I drew them in and out of her.

micah gripped My hand, attempting to remove My fingers from between her toned thighs.

My mouth encircled her erect nipple. I swirled My tongue around her beautiful, dark areola. I traveled across her body, leaving warm, wet kisses on her flesh before giving equal attention to the other breast.

"P-p-please Sir, i'm—i'm close. i'm trying not to come."

I continued to flick My tongue over her left nipple while My fingers worked their magic. "I like this game, micah," I taunted through a mouthful of breast. "you are not to release until I say so."

I removed My fingers from her channel and spread her legs for better access. micah's pussy glistened with her arousal. Fuck. I dove in, lapping away at her creamy center.

I teased micah's swollen clit, goading her and enjoying every moment.

God, she fucking tasted amazing.

micah's hands grasped My hair, trying to push Me away. *Oh no, baby, not yet. I want to keep you on the edge just a little bit longer.* The more she tried to push Me away the more I took that as a challenge. micah would soon learn that the more she attempted to fight Me, the more tortuous things would become for her.

Adding to her torture, I reached up to pinch her nipples while slowly sucking her clit. Using My tongue, I parted her pussy lips before plunging deeper inside of her. There was no stopping the hungry growl that ripped through My chest. Going down on My woman was a big aphrodisiac for Me.

micah was hysterical. she wriggled and thrashed, all with her thighs clamped around My head. This shit was fucking thrilling. I laughed, enjoying the vibration against her sex. That just sent My pretty girl into begging mode. "Please, Sir, please. May i come? Pretty, pretty, pretty please, may i? Please!"

I glanced up to look at her face. her hysteria only heightened My arousal. her eyes were hooded and she looked to be both insanely satisfied and exhausted.

I shifted My body to get a better angle. Oh, the fun was just beginning.

"No, you may not." I wouldn't let her off the hook that easy. I continued My tongue assault while holding micah's wildly bucking hips down. she tried her best to escape My hold.

Spread out on My sheets, wild and begging for release with My face buried in her sweet pussy, micah was so far from the poised professional she portrayed earlier.

she shrieked and pleaded. Tightening her legs around My head and shoulders, she stuttered, "Please, S-S-Sir, please!"

Between her cries of passion and gushing pussy, I was on the verge of losing My load. Coming in My underwear stopped when I was thirteen—no way was that shit ever happening again. I had to maintain self-control.

Ever the Gentleman, I needed to grant micah her release before I even thought about getting off.

"My pretty girl, come for your Master," I said, taking one last lick down her slit.

Watching micah come was a gorgeous sight. she arched her back and completely lost it. Strong tremors erupted from her body as she writhed and whimpered.

her moans were the sweetest sounds.

I was once again thrilled that I was able to get her to squirt. I can't tell you how fucking delightful it was to get a woman so excited that she squirted. I knew My tongue skills were great, but when that happened, it was one hell of a boost to the ego.

I licked up the last bit of her essence before kissing the soft, tender flesh of her inner thighs.

she removed her hands from My hair and rose up on her elbows to watch Me.

My eyes met hers. micah's chest was heaving and her eyes shone brightly in the candlelight.

I continued My trail of kisses up to the juncture of her thighs, releasing a long, contented sigh as I rested My cheek against her hip and closed My eyes.

As micah calmed down, so did I. Our breathing fell into sync, chests rising and falling as if we shared the same lungs.

her hand returned to My head, and her fingers raked through My hair.

I opened My eyes to find My pretty girl examining Me.

"Hi," I whispered, nearly losing Myself in the bottomless depths of her eyes.

her fingers never stopped their soothing massage against My scalp while she stared at Me like I had the answer to all the universe's problems in My eyes; I would give anything for her to always look at Me that way. To look at Me as if she were just as in love with Me as I was with her.

she sighed and spread her lips into a glorious smile. "Hello, Sir."

micah

i love Him. There, i said it.

For the most part, i could detach myself from the act of sex, but with Rick, i couldn't.

They say sex is better when you're in love, and despite kisa's warning to keep my feelings in check, i fell hard and fast. i might regret it later, but for now, i loved Him.

i was madly in love with Rick Thomas, and it only took a few days. Days! Who falls in love in a matter of days? This gal. i was in deep.

i'd never been one of *those* women. Sure, i was the sappy, romantic type, but i hadn't been in many long-term relationships. For one reason or another, every guy i'd dated had never been interested in settling down.

my longest relationship ended a little over a year ago, and since then my dating life had been a bust.

Brent and i were together for three and a half years; it wasn't my first interracial relationship. my philosophy was simple: i was interested in men who were interested in me.

If They happened to be Dominant, even better, but ultimately, a genuine connection mattered more to me than anything else.

Anyhow, Brent and i lived together, but whenever i would mention marriage or next steps in our relationship, he would change the subject. Not to mention i always felt like Brent thought he was doing me a favor by indulging in kink.

He didn't treat me horribly, but sometimes it felt like we were in two separate places.

i dated a lot after college, but Brent was my first real post-college adult relationship. We tried to do what was expected—essentially we played house—but when it came to the next phase, we couldn't close the deal.

Brent was bad for me. i was never fully myself when i was with him, and if there's anyone you should be yourself with, it's your partner. i always got the feeling he judged me for my interests.

Relationships take a lot of effort.

i felt like i gave more time and attention to our relationship than Brent did. i tried to be the doting girlfriend and make it work. i don't believe in simply giving up.

When it came to kink, Brent's lack of interest and sometimes flat-out disgust would make me feel horrible about myself. There was nothing wrong with me liking what i liked and asking my partner to share that with me, but i had always been the one to concede.

We were missing that extra layer of intimacy. That soul-deep connection. We didn't want the same things in or out of the bedroom, but we were familiar. Not necessarily comfortable, but not entirely uncomfortable.

Brent wasn't a bad guy, he just wasn't *the* guy. To prove i had no hard feelings, i was kind enough to stay with kisa for a few days while he packed up his stuff. i didn't think tossing him out of my apartment in anger after years together was the way for us to separate.

In the year since Brent and i broke up and he moved out, i had a series of bad dates and had faced the fact that i probably wouldn't ever find the kind of love i was seeking.

i wanted what i wanted and i was no longer willing to settle. my guard was always up. i would never accept the first Guy who had similar interests. i needed to protect myself.

But then Doctor Rick Thomas appeared out of thin air as my Knight in Shining Armor. He saved me, literally.

Now i was confused.

How do i continue our dynamic without showing my true feelings so soon? We were still in the early stages, but as my training progressed, i knew i'd fall farther down the rabbit hole.

Thankfully, i had the exhibition to keep me occupied. Rick would also be on rotation for the next few days, so i'd have a little bit of breathing room to work out my feelings.

The plan sounded really great in my head.

Deflect, deflect, deflect.

her Master

Weeks passed and My days continued as usual, although I thought about that night at My condo with micah, a lot.

What happened between us was some powerful shit.

I had never felt that strongly about a woman since, well, never. Even samantha and I didn't have the kind of connection that micah and I had already developed.

After several weeks together, neither of us brought up what had transpired that night—the night I firmly declared Myself her Master.

A few days later, a mutually beneficial contract was agreed upon and signed with little reservation. she belonged to Me and I to her. Our journey would surely take us down an exciting path and exceed many expectations.

I looked forward to all our future held. micah gifted Me with her trust, her devotion, and her emotional and spiritual growth. I promised to lead her down an honorable path and be her Protector, her Lover, her Teacher, and her Friend. We were bonded. Of course, she had the freedom to change her mind and ask to be released at any time, but it was My hope that such a thing would never occur.

As micah's training progressed, she proved herself to be everything I could ever have hoped for in a submissive.

As much as I attempted to create a sense of normalcy for our dynamic, My work put Me in a position where I could not turn down requests to cover shifts and lectures. I kept waiting for My pretty girl to crack, but so far she hadn't, even though her training was oftentimes piecemeal.

Guilt had become the prevailing emotion whenever I thought of her; I had to get a handle on My schedule before micah developed feelings of neglect.

What You didn't want was a resentful submissive. I made time for micah as much as possible, but I had to be better. You didn't have a submissive sign a contract if You weren't serious about Your shit. Rules and expectations were written out for a reason.

I hadn't seen micah in person in more than a week, and telephone calls weren't nearly as satisfying. Although My shift had just ended and I was tired, I had to see My pretty girl.

In the time we'd been together, I hadn't once visited micah's apartment, so I hopped a cab across town and headed to Spanish Harlem.

It was completely rude of Me to show up unannounced, but I didn't care. I needed to see her with My own eyes—FaceTime was for the fucking birds. I paid the cabbie and climbed the steps of her building. The brisk breeze had Me eager to wrap Myself in micah's warmth. I rang the buzzer twice and waited. A couple of minutes passed before her voice squeaked out of the silver box.

"Yes? Who is it?"

"micah, it's Me. Ring Me up, please."

"Sir?" she asked, her tone full of surprise. Who wouldn't be surprised at an unexpected visitor at 12:20 a.m. on a weeknight?

Guilt rolled in. I really felt like shit for not calling. Granted, I had the final say in what was acceptable, but it would have been fair to consider micah's evening. What if I had woken her up? What if she had retired early because she had to be at the museum earlier than normal?

Shit!

The museum.

Shit, shit, shit.

Tonight was the opening of her exhibition, and I'd missed it. Goddamnit, I'd missed it.

I couldn't believe I'd gotten so sidetracked. Why didn't micah remind Me? Surely she had to have known I would've made adequate arrangements to attend. At least I hoped she knew. I would've loved to have been there to see My pretty girl shine.

"Yes, micah, it's Me," I replied, trying to keep My tone even despite feeling like a dick.

The buzzer rang, granting Me entry. micah's building was a walk-up, and of course her apartment was located on the top floor of the four-story building. A little cardio after work never hurt. her place was nice, well-maintained, and in a decent part of Spanish Harlem. she chose wisely.

When I arrived at the top floor, I found her apartment door cracked a bit. Ever the Gentleman, I knocked before I entered. she gave Me shit about leaving My door unlocked when I went to fetch her in My lobby, but she did the same in a far less secure building? Oh, we'd be talking about this.

"micah?" I called out, slowly pushing the door open. I expected to be greeted by a sleepy and slightly pissed-off woman, but instead she stood behind the door, using it as some sort of shield.

I couldn't get a good look at her and every time I attempted to move closer, the door swung farther back, blocking her from My advances.

"micah, what's wrong? I apologize for not calling. Were you sleeping? Why didn't you remind Me that tonight was your opening? you know I would have been there, right?"

There was really no excuse, but I needed her to understand. "My days have overlapped. I would have loved to be there and show My support."

I was so concerned with My faux pas that it didn't register that micah wasn't in her presenting position. It did however register that I was talking to her through a fucking door.

her voice was small and muffled. "Sir, i wasn't expecting You to visit. i'm not in a presentable state to greet You. Please forgive me."

she didn't acknowledge My apology for missing her big night, and now she was asking for forgiveness for not being presentable? Something was off.

As stipulated in our contract, micah would be expected to greet Me by kneeling at My feet, resting on her haunches with her palms facedown on her thighs.

"micah, what are you talking about?" I asked. "Why are you not in your presenting position?"

"It's no excuse, but i'm a mess, Sir. i just got home from the museum about an hour ago and i was getting ready for bed. i'm sorry for my appearance," she said, stepping from behind the door.

I laughed. It was a dick move, but I laughed hard.

Little rods peeked out from under the scarf micah had covering her head. she was also bare-faced and wearing an oversize Snoopy T-shirt.

she stood with her head bowed while I chuckled.

I closed and locked the apartment door and made My way over to where she stood. Tilting her chin up, I made her look at Me.

"micah, I'm sorry for laughing. I wasn't expecting to see you this way, but I find it adorable . . ." I gently grabbed her hands and brought them to My lips. "you're adorable."

she gave Me a soft smile, but something in her eyes said she was still uneasy.

"I'll excuse you for not presenting properly. I should've called, sweetheart. I'm actually in the wrong here." I kissed her palms and held her hands to My lips. "Why didn't you remind Me that your exhibition opening was tonight? I would've called in a few favors to get a shift change."

she didn't respond, but her face displayed a look of uneasiness.

"Hey, I can tell something's on your mind. Tell Me what's bothering you. Remember, we agreed to open communication."

"i'm menstruating, Sir. i'm not sure if that's the reason for Your visit tonight, but i am near the end of my cycle. i'm a little later than usual, i guess due to stress. i can provide You with oral services, but i'm unavailable for You in a mutual capacity."

I still hadn't fucked her. Excuse Me, *made love* to her. Ultimately that's what I wanted to do. I ate her pussy regularly and she gave Me some of the best blow jobs I'd ever encountered, but micah and I hadn't yet crossed into territory outside of oral sex.

The Pill was fully effective, and we could forgo condoms if we were at that stage, but after eight weeks, I still wasn't ready. No matter how much My dick willed it to happen. I had no desire to *just* fuck her.

"I'm not here for that, and I remembered your cycle was around this time, sweetheart. At least I remembered that. I've just been swamped, but I wanted to see you, to hold you. My shift ended a little while ago and all I want to do is take a shower and fall asleep with you beside Me. I really do feel guilty about stopping by so late and missing your big event."

she bit her lower lip.

We usually slept in the same bed after something of a sexual nature occurred, so for Me to show up without wanting anything but to sleep next to her—I think it scared the shit out of her. Hell, it scared Me. she was the only person I constantly thought about.

"That sounds nice. After the evening i've had, i would love to be held."

"Do you want to talk about it?" I asked.

she stood looking down at her feet, tugging on the hem of her T-shirt. My eyes were drawn to the Snoopy graphic as I waited for her response.

"Perhaps we can talk about it later, after You've had some time to relax as well. May i take Your jacket, Sir?"

I shrugged out of My jacket and handed it to her. she hung it in the hallway closet before showing Me around. Sad that this was the first time I saw where My pretty girl laid her head when she wasn't with Me.

The cozy one-bedroom home fit micah to a tee. The décor, bohemian chic with a vintage edge, mirrored her personality.

"Would You like something to drink, Sir? Or something to eat?"

Almost one in the morning and the little vixen was all about seeing if I was satisfied. That's My girl.

"No, I'm fine for now. I'd just like to shower. If you could leave a glass of water by the bed for Me, that would be preferred."

"Yes, Sir. As You saw, the bathroom is down the hall. i'll go get You a towel," she said, walking into her bedroom.

That damn Snoopy T-shirt was the cutest thing I'd seen in a while. Amazing. Even completely dressed down, I still found micah sexy as hell, roller rods and all. Yeah, I had it bad.

Some people were wary of falling in love with their submissives, but I wasn't one of those types.

I wanted love.

I wanted to love only her.

So why hadn't I said those three words yet? It wasn't "too soon." You feel how You feel. Love had no timetable. I couldn't condense love into a flow chart. Love couldn't be dissected and replicated. It was wild and unique for each of us.

I guess I hesitated because I wanted the words to just roll off My tongue.

Whenever I confessed My feelings, the sentiment would be organic, absolute, and reciprocated.

I had a lot on My mind and spent the entire time in the shower thinking too hard.

After a long day, My muscles relaxed as the hot droplets rolled down My skin. Everything here was micah-size. Washing up was a challenge. If My big body wasn't knocking over body washes and loofahs, I was getting tangled in the shower curtain.

micah tapped on the door. "i brought Your towel, Sir." her voice held a remnant of laughter. she must have heard Me fumbling in here.

I peeked My shampoo-covered head out of the shower. "Thank you." Water and soap threatened to get into My eyes. I reached up to brush the moisture from My face, nearly knocking the shower rod off with My elbow.

micah let out a squeak and then gaped at Me, all previous amusement dried up.

"I'll be in the bedroom in a few minutes," I said before turning to dip My head under the spray.

I toweled off and righted everything I'd disturbed in micah's bathroom before realizing I had nothing to wear. Fuck. And micah had collected My discarded clothing before she scurried away. Oh well, it's not like I hadn't slept in the nude before.

Tonight was different. We'd be in micah's bed. she'd seen Me in the buff on numerous occasions—this shouldn't be any different—but micah could be skittish. It was best to let her set the rules for her home, but I wasn't going to say anything if she didn't.

With the towel snugly wrapped around My waist, I headed to the bedroom. micah was already tucked under the covers and had her back to Me. I removed the towel from around My waist and hung

112

it on the knob of her closet door before slipping under the covers and pulling her body close to Me. "you awake, pretty girl?" I whispered.

"Yes, Sir."

I wrapped My arms around her waist and listened to her breathe.

"micah, this was what I needed tonight. *you* are exactly what I needed," I whispered while kissing the back of her scarf-covered head. I inhaled her sweet scent, a mixture of lemon and lavender.

"i'm glad i could provide You with comfort, Sir."

"That you did. I really am sorry about tonight, sweetheart. I doubt I could ever apologize enough to assuage My guilt. Did everything go over well?"

"Yes. For the most part, yes, things went well. i'm honestly glad it's over."

I heard what she was saying but it was hard for Me to concentrate on her words. I kept thinking about how good it felt to have her in My arms. I wanted this every day.

With My schedule, it was impossible to see micah daily, but I had an idea. An idea that could benefit us both but would also give Me unfettered access to My pretty girl.

"micah, look at Me."

she slipped out of My embrace, turning her body to face Me. "Yes, Sir?" she replied.

"Move in with Me."

she looked at Me wide-eyed. Not exactly the reaction I was expecting, but okay. . . .

"i-i'm sorry, Sir, will You please repeat that?"

"Move in with Me, micah."

There was a brief pause before she stammered out a reply. "i-i-i can't, Sir."

Definitely wasn't anticipating that. It would've been nice if her shooting Me down hadn't come so quickly.

I tried not to sound too hurt. "And why can't you? In our contract, you had no opposition to us living together. What's the problem now that I'm presenting you with the opportunity?" Pain twisted in My gut, forming a knot of frustration.

"i'd have no opposition to living with You if i were collared, Sir."

Oh, I was getting agitated. What the fuck? Was she serious? Living arrangements were explicitly discussed in our contract. Correction, I wasn't agitated—I was fucking livid.

"What do you think the end game is here? Why do you think I'm doing this?" I responded as calmly as possible.

"But i'm not collared, Sir. Not to mention i'm a bit wary of the proposal."

I quirked My brow at her last statement. "What's that supposed to mean? Speak freely, micah, and hold nothing back."

"i like my apartment, Sir. i've been in Spanish Harlem for the last six years. my rent is stabilized, which is unheard of in this day and age, and i like my neighborhood. i'm not sure i'm ready to give that up without a collar or another type of commitment."

"By 'another type of commitment,' I'm assuming you mean marriage?"

"Yes. i also wonder why You want me to move in with You. Why now? Isn't it a bit too soon?"

I was pissed. While everything seemed like a great idea in My mind, it was clear I wasn't really thinking things through.

micah had very good questions and I wanted to be able to give her some decent answers. The concept of time was important in some instances, yet had absolutely no relevance in others. You couldn't fit feelings into a box. You also couldn't turn the motherfuckers off. They came and You dealt with them. Nothing about what was developing between micah and I fit into a neat box.

Our relationship was accelerated because of My feelings. I was trying My best to pump the brakes and let things occur naturally, but I could be a pretty impatient Guy.

she deserved an answer despite My exasperation. "micah, as much as I try to control it, My work schedule is unpredictable. I'm working on making it better, but I don't like stretches of time where we only can keep in contact via text messages, FaceTime, and phone conversations. That's the best way to doom what we have going here."

I stroked her cheek as she hung on My every word. Those brown eyes of hers held so much hope. I wanted her to understand why I wanted her with Me. Why I needed her.

"I want you to move in because I want you close to Me. When I go to bed, when I wake up, I want you near."

micah hesitated before speaking. I loved that she was trying to be careful with her words, but I wanted to hear them without her tiptoeing around with tact.

"Go on, micah."

"i understand Your point, Sir, but um . . ."

"you can speak freely, micah, there's no need to feel that you can't express yourself."

she bit her lip. From her facial expression and continued hesitation, she was clearly thinking of how to best phrase her next statement. "Don't You think it's too soon, Sir, to want that kind of commitment? me living with You? i'd have to give up my apartment. i know You're very balanced when it comes to decision-making, but respectfully, i don't see how that's fair."

she was right, and what she asked made a lot of sense, which is why I had already thought about My plan of action.

"you're right, micah, it is one-sided, so let Me offer an addendum—I do believe in being fair."

I raised My brow, and she followed suit. Oh, there was that feisty I loved so much.

"you move in with Me and I'll pay the rent and utilities on your apartment for six months so you can keep it. Six months should be a good enough trial period to decide if this is something you want to do permanently. If, at the end of six months, you're still uncertain, we can revisit the terms again. How does that sound?"

To Me it sounded fucking perfect, but I was more interested in what My pretty girl thought.

"May i ask a question first, Sir?"

"you may."

"Doctors make good salaries, but depending on the field of study, that salary fluctuates. You're an Attending Physician in the emergency department and an Assistant Professor. How is it that You are able to afford Your place, and now You're offering to pay six months of my rent and utilities? Your condo isn't small. Your neighborhood isn't cheap. You don't exactly live frugally."

she possessed a look of defiance as the last couple of words escaped her lips. "Please tell me it's not due to anything illegal, Sir. i don't want to be associated with anyone involved in illegal activity."

I smirked. Smart line of questioning and valid. One thing I quickly learned about micah: she was very observant. she had a knack for watching and then later, when I least expected it, bringing up what was on her mind when the opportunity presented itself. I'm sure she wanted to ask about My salary sooner but there was never a time for us to discuss it in detail.

"There's nothing illegal happening. I earn a decent salary as a physician, but you're right. I wouldn't be able to afford My home, your rent and utilities, and My lifestyle in general on just that salary alone. you want the truth? Truth is, I'm a trust-fund kid . . . well, actually, My brother and I are trust-fund kids. My father is a retired neurosurgeon and My mother is an heiress. It's not information I tend to share freely, but My mother's side of the family's wealth was acquired via a fleet of newspapers purchased in the mid-1800s. She's not exactly a Rupert Murdoch type, but My mother's shrewd business decisions over the years has ensured the family's legacy continues. I guess you could say I've always had a silver spoon in My mouth, but I've never used it to My advantage. My parents always kept My brother and I grounded."

micah let out a long breath. Wow, I guess she really did suspect that I was involved in some underhanded shit. Glad to clear up any misconceptions, but I wish she had asked Me about this sooner since it clearly bothered her.

she smiled at Me, her eyes somewhat hooded, indicating sleep was beckoning her.

"Luckily, Thomas is My mother's married name, so she can remain under the radar unless some nosy reporter happens to snap her photo and she ends up in the Sunday *Times* or the *Wall Street Journal.* I worked hard to prove I was capable of many things without money or prestige giving Me an advantage. I worked two jobs and had a lot of late nights in order to put Myself through medical school. I wanted normalcy. I wanted to know what hard work was. I became a Doctor because I wanted to make a difference and not be some suit whose only contact with those in need is by writing a check once a year. I mean, I give generously to My favorite charities, but I'm a hands-on kind of Guy. So you see, micah, I never have to work a day in My life, but I choose to because it makes Me happy. Having you move in with Me would also make Me happy. Very happy, actually."

she stared at My chest as I stroked her cheek. "Oh," she replied.

My brow rose at her tone. "Oh?"

"i'm not sure what else i can say, Sir. It's not every day a sub hears her . . . her . . . her Master declare He's well-off."

she finally said it. micah called Me her Master, and My heart fucking swelled. Good girl.

she'd been hesitant and I wondered why. micah had never been in a serious long-term D/s relationship. I chalked up her lack of addressing Me as her Master to her level of comfort. I told her I would never demand anything from her, and I meant it. Respect was always earned, always.

"I guess one could say that, but I don't view Myself that way. My money is tied up in investments and a variety of accounts collecting interest, but I don't rely on it. I live within My means. My condo is My biggest expense. That's the only time I've used My trust fund—to purchase My dream home, design it to My specifications, and furnish it as I saw fit. It's My pride and joy and I'd like to share it with you."

"Can i be honest, Sir?" she replied.

"Of course you can; it's what I always prefer."

"i'm no slouch. i'm pretty headstrong and i can hold my own, but You're intimidating. Although we've been in our dynamic for a bit and i enjoy our time together, i'm still confused as to why You even want me. i realize i have a lot to offer a Man but knowing what i know about You, i don't get why You're asking me to move in.

There are so many others You could have. i'm so far outside the scope of what You're probably used to that i have to wonder, why me?"

I stared at her hard. Was she fucking serious? Not this shit *again*.

micah was a goddamn spitfire, but right then she was somewhere in between attitudinal and self-deprecating, and I didn't like it one bit.

she was amazing. Why the hell wouldn't I choose her? Women. I never could fully figure them out.

I didn't just choose her, she chose Me as well. This wasn't one-sided.

"I told you, micah, I want your face to be the first and last thing I see every single day. I don't care about other submissives and what they may or may not be doing. I only care about what *you're* doing. i find you beautiful. you have a beautiful spirit. you're hardworking, you're kind, you're playful, your intellect keeps Me on My toes. you intrigue Me like no other. Are those enough reasons?" I'm sure My tone had some bite to it, but I wanted her to stop the doubt.

"Yes."

"Yes?"

"Yes, Sir, i agree to accept the terms of the trial run. Six months it is."

I kissed her forehead before My lips parted in a wide grin.

"I'll hire movers in the morning."

I kissed her forehead again before she turned in My arms and My warm body covered hers.

"Are you ready to go sleep?"

"Yes i am. So very ready."

"Good night, micah."

"Good night, Master."

This—this is exactly what I wanted for the rest of My life.

micah

It was strange knowing that in a matter of days i'd wake up to my Master every morning. His presence had been missed in my home despite Him leaving a little more than twenty-four hours ago. He'd left that morning under oath that He would handle everything.

True to His word, movers were waiting outside my apartment building when i hit the curb to leave for work the following morning.

He wasn't joking.

i assumed i'd have at least a few more days to wrap my head around this, but my Master had other ideas. This was a huge step and marked the beginning of our life together. Well, the six-month trial run of our life together.

While i was at work, the movers spent the majority of the day packing up my apartment. The furniture, cookware, dinnerware, and kitchen appliances remained but everything else went to my Master's condo.

A variety of thoughts weaved their way through my mind— mainly, how bad my last attempt at cohabitation had failed. i kept reminding myself that this was different. Sir was different. i knew there was no comparison. i tried not to think too hard about it as i handed a box of my belongings to the movers.

This was it. my apartment was now sterile. i was going to miss my cozy haven, but i was excited for the next phase of our relationship.

We'd been living together for almost two months but we'd been in our dynamic for twice as long. Things had been going well, we were good partners, but i was frustrated beyond belief. He hadn't touched me sexually other than oral sex.

Well, my Master *was* proficient in oral sex, and with those damn clit vibrators. On one of the rare occasions we attended a private party, Sir exposed me to a few new and exhilarating experiences . . . and my nemesis.

When we entered the loft, my Master rested His hands on my shoulders and pulled my coat off, handing it to a sub who was working at the coat check. The clatter of the party rose and bounced off the high ceilings. There were so many people, most of whom had turned their focus on Rick once we stepped farther into the loft. There were a few Men and Women who greeted Him with congratulatory handshakes and claps on the back. *Congratulations, it's a sub!* Our contract had been finalized months ago, yet this was the first time we'd been to a private party. Sir and i had spent the past several weeks, when we weren't buried in work, with our faces buried in each other's laps.

"Are You going to show her off tonight?" a Man who seemed vaguely familiar asked Rick as if goading Him.

my Master's hand pressed against the small of my back, urging me forward. "micah, this is Master Otho."

i kept my eyes downcast until Rick placed my hand in the other Man's. When i looked up, recognition dawned, and my face must have shown it if Master Otho's warm laughter was an indication. Master Otho was married to Mistress Sybil, and together they were *the* preeminent lifestyle couple in the tri-state area. i'd seen pictures—highly staged pictures—but people look much different in person.

"she is lovely, Master Rick. Sybil and the others are eager to see how micah's training has been progressing." Master Otho shot a look at Sir and then brought my hand to His lips. "Welcome, micah."

"Thank You, Sir."

Rick and Master Otho led me through the party, stopping every few feet to be introduced to other Dominants and Their subs or slaves.

In public, the differences between a submissive and slave were more stark. Yes, no one was to approach me without my Dom's permission, and Sir had the definitive say in what we did, but i was still very much my own person in this dynamic and could function independently of Him. We had established very clear rules in our contract but were open enough with each another to leave room for our relationship to grow and change. my Master firmly and lovingly guided me to and through new situations. Some experiences were more successful than others, and Rick had no issues making adjustments when things might have gone too far for either of us.

The slaves, both men and women, we were introduced to had to be told to greet us or take a drink and so on. their Dominants dictated every single moment when they were together.

i admitted to having *some* slave tendencies; however, Rick did not have full authority over *every* aspect of my life. i didn't want that, and i didn't believe a 24/7 Total Power Exchange was something He'd ever been interested in. It would mean that as His slave, i would have no rights or say-so whatsoever. While my goal was always to serve Him and make sure His needs were met, i enjoyed the freedom of making my own decisions.

While i would never knock a sub or slave for their choices, that extreme simply wasn't right for the D/s dynamic Rick and i had developed over these past couple of months.

We sat on a low sofa with another couple who were enamored with Sir. Everyone we spoke to addressed Him as "Master." The level of respect and admiration that swelled around Him was a bit intimidating.

my Master ran His hand up and down my spine and then drew me closer to His side. "Are you enjoying yourself, sweetheart?" He whispered in my ear, making me shiver.

i nodded. "Yes, Sir, but it's all so different from the playroom," i answered while watching Mistress Sybil and Master Otho move to the center of the room.

"you've been doing so well, micah. May I show you off a little bit?"

He knew i wasn't very much into public scening, but He really wanted this.

"Yes, Sir."

my Master stood and extended His hand, pulling me to my feet. He led me to the center of the room where He then whispered something to Mistress Sybil. She stepped away, winking at me before disappearing behind a screen.

Master Otho stepped away as well, but returned to hand Rick a cord of rope.

Taking His time, my Master placed me in a variety of positions that allowed Him to drag the rope over my skin, forming intricate knots. He bound my limbs with care, forming the knots on erotic pressure points. The roughness ignited an even more powerful response than the silk scarves He used when we were in the playroom. The feeling of the natural fiber on my skin was heavenly. All of this was new to me. i had never experienced Shibari but always wanted to. i had no idea it was an interest of Sir's.

i tried not to cry out from both the pain and pleasure i found in the scratch and pinch of the rope. To be bound in such a way was both terrifying and freeing. my Master satisfied my curiosity about rope bondage and gave me one of the most amazing experiences i had ever encountered. Well, an amazing experience until my high was quickly crushed by the taunting of a clit vibrator.

That fucking thing—evil but oh so pleasurable. The taunting lasted for at least thirty minutes before He finally granted me release.

We'd done so much, had come so far, but it had been almost five months and nothing. . . .

Ugh.

Not once had He ever initiated sexual intercourse.

i kept expecting it. i kept waiting for it. i wanted it, but it never happened.

i was eager to broach the topic but wasn't exactly sure how to address it. Our contract stated that my Master and i would have sex whenever He saw fit, with the exception of the five days each month i had my period.

Of course, i was horny even during my most unsexy time. i had nothing but dick on the brain.

Wake up, dick.

Shower, dick.

Eat breakfast, dick.

Get the picture?

my longing renewed each time His tongue would lave my cream and His fingers would penetrate my delicate flower.

Despite my Master getting off and getting me off night after night, i would go to bed unfulfilled.

Here i was, curled up under a hunk of a Man who wouldn't fuck me. i'm an attractive woman, but i began to question if i turned Him on. It definitely did something to my self-esteem.

my negative thoughts were sometimes silenced by the way Rick would eye me as if He were a predator waiting to devour me. Those looks often tempered my anxiety.

i was patient, but if this kept up, i feared i might die from lack of penetration. While there had been no reported cases of any such thing happening, i think i was on target to becoming the first casualty.

my Master drew circles around my belly button with His finger as we lay in bed. Although we didn't have sex, we did just have an incredibly satisfying experience.

my eyes drifted closed at the contentment that enveloped us.

"My nephews really want to meet you," He said with His head pillowed on my breast, "so I promised everyone we'd spend the holiday at mom and dad's."

Since we'd been living together, it wasn't often that Rick *told* me what we were doing. It was well within His rights as my Dom, but He almost always asked my opinion.

Truly, there was nothing to object to, but it would have been nice to be asked if i were ready to meet the rest of the Thomas family.

"What kind of things do they like? Should i come bearing gifts?"

my Master's laughter vibrated the bed. "Caleb and William are seven and nine and the spawn of the Devil himself."

"Don't say that. i bet they're wonderful boys."

"you haven't met My brother. I don't know how Steph—God bless her—puts up with Todd and his more evil mini-Todds."

i sat up to give Him a stern look. "i can't believe You," i said through a laugh, swatting His shoulder.

"you know I adore those brats, sweetheart, but somebody's gotta keep it real with them. That's what uncle Rick is for."

"Uncle Rick, huh?" i liked that. Sighing, i laid back down and raked my fingers through my Master's hair and drifted off to sleep.

Thanksgiving Day had arrived. If i thought the nerves i experienced during my exhibition opening were bad, this was unbelievably worse.

i stood in front of our bedroom mirror attaching a plum-colored pendant around my neck before putting the final touches on my makeup. my eyes tracked my Master in the mirror as He stepped out of the bathroom, making His way toward me.

Rick was the epitome of sleek.

A well-dressed Man was universally sexy, and my Master had sexiness down to a science. He donned a pair of navy dress pants and a crisp, white button-down shirt. In His left hand He held a medium-size black velvet box and in the other, a gray tie with hints of blue. His silver cuff links shone, completing the ensemble.

With a quizzical expression, i turned around to face Him. "Sir, may i ask what's in the box?"

He ignored my question and gently set the black box on the dresser before handing me His tie. "Would you help Me with My tie, micah?"

"Of course," i replied, biting my lip. Now i was even more curious. i tried to concentrate on making sure to form the perfect knot, but i was distracted by the presence of the velvet box.

He tried horribly to suppress a smirk; a playful Rick was always fun. He knew i was intrigued.

i finished tying the knot and smoothed out His shirt, my hands lingering on His defined pecs. "All done, Sir. It's perfect," i said, preparing to step away and return to my makeup.

He halted my progress, slipping His arms around my waist and pulling me closer to Him.

"you look beautiful, micah. My family is going to love you," He whispered in my ear.

my God, i felt my pussy clench with need. It didn't take much, but He always knew how to raise my body temperature way past ninety-eight-point-six degrees.

"Thank You, Sir. You look very handsome as well," i countered.

He ran His tongue slowly up and down my neck, nipping at my earlobe before planting small kisses along my jawline.

my breathing hitched and my eyes rolled into the back of my head as His hands gripped me tighter around my waist.

"you're curious about what's in the box?" He asked, slowly kissing the pulse point on my neck.

i bit my lip to suppress a moan.

i wanted to scream. He had a habit of building up my excitement only to leave me unfulfilled. Here i was fidgeting like a bitch in heat, but He remained calm, cool, and collected.

i may have been celibate for a longer amount of time, but my Master hadn't had sex in months. *Months.* That's like forty dog years for a Man with a healthy libido. He had unfettered access to my body and He never took full advantage.

i couldn't understand it. What Man would willingly put Himself through such a torture? More importantly, *why* would a Man put Himself through such torture?

"We're going to have some fun tonight. What I have in the box is for both of us, micah."

i didn't like His tone—not at all. There was an underlying mischief present. It was only a matter of time before the other shoe dropped.

He released me from His hold before walking over to the dresser to scoop up the velvet box. Extending the box to me, He said, "Here, open your gift."

i looked up at Him, trying to read His facial expression, but He gave nothing away. my Master simply gave me one of His trademark smirks and folded His arms across His broad chest. The way His dress shirt stretched across His pecs induced all sorts of naughty images.

i was so close to begging to be fucked.

Before opening the box, i glanced at Him once more, hoping that His facial expression would give me some sort of clue as to what was inside.

"Go ahead," He instructed, putting His hands in His pockets. *Sexy motherfucker.*

i opened the box to discover a love egg staring back at me. i looked up to see Him twirling the wireless remote around His finger.

i had no words, none. He couldn't possibly want me to put this thing inside me and wear it to Thanksgiving dinner with His family. No way in hell. He wouldn't be that cruel, would He?

He couldn't be serious. . . .

Just as i was about to inquire, my Master stepped closer, His massive body practically on top of me, and somehow got closer still before detailing His plan. His voice low and smooth, His words devastating. "you'll insert the egg before we depart. My intention is to make you come very hard all while not disturbing our meal. Do you understand?"

i nodded.

"you know better. A verbal response, please, micah."

"Yes, Master, whatever You desire," i replied softly.

Shit. He never indicated that He was a Sadist of sorts. Okay, maybe calling Him a Sadist was a bit extreme, but this was fucked up.

Oh, it's a pleasure to meet you, Mr. and Mrs. Thomas. Please excuse me while i come all over your Queen Anne chair.

i take that back. Rick was a Sadist to demand this of me. For all that was dear and holy, why?

i wanted to cry. my pussy wanted to cry. we were both miserable.

i quickly closed the box and returned to the mirror to apply a bit more blush before i was instructed to insert that horrid apparatus. my back was to Him, but i could see His reflection in the mirror as He stood behind me.

"Do you like it?" He asked, watching me apply translucent powder to my cheekbones. "Somehow, I thought you'd find the color pink appealing."

"Yes, Sir," i lied.

Shit. i don't know why i said yes, He'd know in an instant i didn't mean it.

"micah," He replied sternly, "don't lie to Me. you know how I feel about dishonesty."

Yep, it was really futile to feign delight. He saw through me every time. i had to to come clean. "The pink is fine, Sir. Honestly, i'm fine with the color. i'm just not thrilled with . . ."

"With what?" He asked, making His way toward me.

i whispered, "With us."

He frowned. He had always asked that i be truthful, but i wasn't so sure He wanted to hear this truth.

His voice wavered before becoming quieter. "What do you mean, you're not thrilled with us?" my Master's face ran through about a million different emotions in less than a breath before teetering between hurt and anger. "Don't tell Me you want to back out . . ."

On some level i was glad for His strong reaction. He made me feel like that almost every day.

i didn't want to leave Him—there was no way in the world i could walk away from Him. Things were close to perfect between us, except for that one area of contention.

"No, i'm not backing out, Sir. i really don't . . . i-i'm a bit confused and need some clarity."

Rick raised an eyebrow and crossed His arms over His chest. "Clarity about what, exactly?"

i had His attention, so i needed to woman up and tell my Master what was troubling me.

"Well, i had been wondering why You haven't initiated anything beyond oral sex with me. We've been together for some time now, and neither of us have had other partners since we began our relationship." my heart pounded against my rib cage, pushing me to say more. "You wanted monogamy and exclusivity. You have both. i have a clean bill of health. i'm on the Pill. i've moved in here." i counted off all of His requirements on my fingers, never taking my eyes off His.

Something flickered there. Doubt? Remorse?

i shouldn't have said that. . . .

He blinked, and whatever insecurities Rick had shown vanished. my Master pressed His lips together and nodded for me to continue.

i swallowed and lowered my gaze. "You're well aware of everything i've said, Sir. They were all things we agreed upon in our contract. So forgive me, but i just don't understand. Have i done something to displease You?" i wrapped my arms around myself, feeling small and stupid for putting so much stock in a sex act, but damnit, i wanted Him. i had uprooted my life because i trusted Him and the connection i believed we shared.

He demanded honesty. Well, i deserved some too.

"i've been a really good, patient girl. i was under the impression that one of the reasons i'd be moving in with You was to ramp up our intimacy level, but You never touch me . . . *like that.*" Looking up, i met His penetrating stare. The blue of His irises flickered again, this time the softness lingered.

He sighed loudly before approaching me and gently cupping my face in His hands. "micah, trust Me when I say that I find you attractive in every way. you are physically and intellectually stunning. you keep Me on My toes. you're confident, you're sensitive, you're attentive, you're driven, you're independent. you're the bright spot in My life, pretty girl. I'm very content with you. Actually, I'm more than content with you."

His words and His actions were contradictory. We lived together. We shared a bed every night. If i was everything He said i was to Him, then why didn't my Master want to increase our level of intimacy?

"If i'm all the things You say i am, then why haven't we made love, Sir?" i asked.

He owed me the truth, even if it hurt. i wanted to hear it. i deserved to hear it.

He paused briefly as if He were carefully selecting His words. "Please, micah. I just need time. I know it's selfish for Me to ask that of you, but I need you to trust Me on this."

He needed time?

i sacrificed. i was fully invested in making this dynamic work. i signed a contract and freely gave myself to Him. i agreed to uproot my life and move in with Him to see if what we had was sustainable for the long run.

i was looking for forever.

He occupied my mind and my spirit.

On numerous occasions, when we would lay together, i poured my soul out to Him regarding my dreams and my desires. i loved Him. i was in love with Him. So what if i hadn't told Him yet? i knew what i felt.

But He needed time. Time? What the fuck could He possibly need more time for?

my hands began to shake as He caressed my face. i was livid. i didn't give a fuck about repercussions. i no longer cared about knowing my place. Decorum went out the fucking window.

There had to be a reason He was stalling.

i blurted out the first thing that came to mind. "Are You still in love with samantha? Is that what's keeping You from having sex with me? Do You still have feelings for her?"

i was silently praying He'd say no.

If He admitted He was still in love with samantha, i think my heart would shatter. i had invested so much in this relationship and was on a path to regret.

kisa was right. i should've listened to her when i had the chance to walk away unscathed.

Before, i saw what i wanted. i wanted to believe Rick and i had a connection. i wanted to believe that He felt as strongly about me as i did about Him. i took His words at face value because He had asked me to trust Him. And i did trust Him.

He had seemed so earnest, and now He was asking me to trust Him again.

i had no reason to trust Him. His desire to treat me as a plaything spoke volumes. i wasn't worth fucking. Why did He even bother asking me to meet His family? What was the point?

He guffawed before slipping His hands from my face and placing them on my waist. His laugh quickly subsided as He stared at me with an intensity i'd never witnessed before.

His normally bright blue eyes darkened. The look He gave me made it clear that i'd hit a sore spot. A very, very sore spot. He looked as angry as i felt.

Well then, now we're even. Why be offended because i spoke the truth?

"This," He said through clenched teeth while gesturing between us, "doesn't have shit to do with samantha. she isn't a factor. she has never been a factor. Ever. I just need time. Please, give Me that, micah. I know it's a lot to ask of you, but you have to understand that if I'm asking you to be patient it's for a very good reason."

He cupped my face in His hands. "Please," He whispered, resting His forehead against mine.

i wriggled out of His grasp. "Sure, Sir. Time. If that's what You seek, i'll give You time," i responded tersely.

i was certain He picked up the brusqueness in my tone. i have never blatantly disrespected a Dom. Never once. But now i didn't care. i was pissed.

i'm sure he was bothered by my tone but He didn't call me on it.

i was ready to end this conversation. i didn't want to hear anymore, but Rick didn't want to let it go.

He pulled me closer to Him as i tried my best to move away. i didn't want to be anywhere near Him at that moment but He held my wrists as He spoke. "micah, please don't be upset. Know that I find you incredibly desirable. We'll get there, pretty girl, I promise. Now, go insert your egg so we can test it out and be on our way."

He fucking had to be kidding, right?

i couldn't give two shits about the egg.

Inside, i was a volcano ready to explode. i wanted to cry. i had so much i wanted to say, but i bit my tongue. i wanted to give Him a piece of my mind and call bullshit on His claim of finding me desirable.

How does that even make sense? Actions speak louder than words, right? At that moment, i felt like i was getting a lot of lip service.

With a hefty dose of attitude, i promptly turned on my heels and headed into the bathroom with that godforsaken egg in tow.

i didn't know what to do, but i knew for certain i didn't want to give Him time.

Fuck Your time.

she was pissed.

micah had remained respectful, barely—and I do mean *barely*.

Normally, I would never tolerate such insolence from a submissive, but I could see by looking at her a battle was waging within. I allowed her brazenness because I understood her frustration.

micah was granted one freebie and that was it.

Funny thing was, it was a turn-on to witness micah's poor attempts at controlling her anger.

I couldn't blame her for being angry. How would I even explain to her what I was thinking without making her feel like shit?

Sorry, micah, I don't want to have sex with you until I can tell you I love you. I'm certain I do, but I guess I have cold feet when it comes to saying the words.

Charming, right?

My emotional connection with micah was pretty profound; it even surprised Me sometimes.

When she wasn't angry with Me, we had a tendency to finish each other's sentences. I laughed at the corniest things due to her silly sense of humor. she loved everything about the '80s while I cringed thinking about the tacky trends that stemmed from that time in history. Don't get Me wrong, I loved a lot of the music that came out of the '80s, but the majority of things from that decade I could do without.

she had this hilarious habit of cooking My breakfast in only her underwear while lip-syncing to that song "Maniac" from *Flashdance*. Quirky and weird and completely at ease with herself, that was part of what drew Me to her. she was perfect in every sense of the word. micah didn't attempt to impress anyone. she was a woman comfortable in her skin, and I found that to be an incredible turn-on.

At times, when she wasn't aware of My presence, I would watch her. I swear My heart beat a little faster. What I had with micah was rare.

I was a lucky Man, a truly lucky Man.

Thanksgiving dinner went off without a hitch, even after the prequel to World War III. Well, if you didn't count the four times I cranked the wireless remote to the egg up to its highest setting. By My estimate, micah came three, possibly four times, and that was all before dessert was served.

Oh, My pretty girl fought hard to control her demeanor and did a hell of a job. No one seemed to notice how uncomfortable she was, despite her occasional fits of stuttering.

I was having a bit of a difficult time controlling My lust.

micah had the best O face. It was even more spectacular when she was trying desperately not to embarrass herself. It was fucked up, but I reveled in watching her squirm.

Hopefully, this was a lesson learned. she needed to get a handle on how to better control her emotions. It was probably cruel of Me to test her limits in the company of My family, but seeing micah—who was usually the epitome of poise—unravel did something to Me. Since she was clearly angry, I figured, why not taunt her a little more?

In some instances, I found it pleasurable observing micah in uncomfortable predicaments. her level of discomfort this evening rivaled when we returned to Spanxxx for a fun night out on the town. Unbeknownst to her, I had volunteered us for a sensation play demo that illustrated the wonders of the Wartenberg wheel. Good times, man, good times.

micah had never been much for scening in public, so that night at Spanxxx truly came as a surprise. Public play was one of her soft limits I continually pushed.

We'd indulged in public scenes a handful of times, and despite her unease, she had always been obedient, for the most part, but there were times when she had been bratty. Bratty behavior and I didn't mix, and micah had learned it wouldn't be tolerated. A few swats on her ass with a rattan cane served as a great behavior modification tool.

Ultimately, micah always did as she was told. Let Me clarify here: I didn't do things to simply make her abide to *My* desires. I liked to push her so that she would be able to grow. A bird wouldn't take flight until it felt confident in its ability. micah was My bird, she was soaring towards greatness, and the longer we were together the better she would become. Trust Me when I tell you I would never have done anything detrimental to her well-being—I'm not that kind of Man.

So back to Thanksgiving dinner: The table was filled with endless chatter and many embarrassing stories of My youth. My nephews updated Me on their school woes and sports interests. I glanced at micah numerous times throughout dinner and even squeezed her hand underneath the table to assure her that I was proud of her.

Initially, I was greeted with a scowl, but soon her lips turned upward into the most beautiful smile. her smile lit up the room. she appeared to be enjoying the food and conversation, and from what I could tell, My parents loved micah. They asked a variety of questions about her interests, her job, her family, and of course, how we met.

I knew this was My mother's way of getting back at Me for not bringing micah around sooner. Surprise over Me bringing a guest was to be expected, not the Family Feud version of "Get to Know micah" at the dinner table. But then again, I should have anticipated it; Lena Thomas always marched to the beat of her own drummer. My dad and Todd attempted to interject a few times to take the focus off of micah, but when My mother was on a mission, forget about it.

micah managed to make it through the conversation unscathed and appeared genuinely happy answering everyone's questions. she handled My family with ease, and I was proud of her for keeping her cool.

After dinner, micah remained in the living room looking through old family photo albums with My sister-in-law and nephews while My dad and Todd watched the football game. My family's interest in the Dallas Cowboys was borderline obsessive. I was a Cowboys fan, born and raised. Thomas Men have always supported them, but I wasn't much in the mood for football or a trip down memory lane. I slipped into the kitchen to see if My mother needed any assistance.

My mom was humming as she donned her oven mitts to remove the pumpkin pies from the oven. "Micah seems lovely. I have to say, I was surprised you brought a guest. You haven't brought anyone around since Samantha." How the hell did she know it was Me? Did she have eyes in the back of her head?

I guess there really was something to that woman's intuition thing. I cringed when she mentioned *her* name. I knew it was coming at some point this evening; it was inevitable. But damnit, why the hell did she have to mention sam?

"I know, Mom. There really hasn't been anyone worth bringing around until micah. I haven't been seeing anyone seriously until now."

"How long have you two been together?"

"Almost five months."

"And she's living with you already? That's pretty fast, wouldn't you say?" My mother inquired, raising an eyebrow as she placed the pies on the cooling rack. I knew that look. My mother had many things she wasn't saying.

Might as well get it all out and clear the air. Nothing like a holiday gathering to bring out the confessions and unfiltered conversation. That's what holidays were for, right? Some turkey and stuffing, a little family meddling in Your love life, the passing of the cranberry sauce.

Fine, I'd bite. I might as well get it out of the way. There was no sense in delaying the imminent prying that was sure to occur.

"Why do I feel like there's something you're not saying, Mom?"

"She's black. I was a bit surprised. She's an attractive young lady, but I hadn't anticipated you being in an interracial relationship. You never mentioned it when you said you were bringing a guest to dinner."

I felt My eye twitch. I didn't know if I should be angry or if I should've anticipated what My mother had said. As far as I knew, she didn't have a racist bone in her body. My parents never expressed any negativity towards other races and ethnicities. She was only voicing what I was sure many people in our family would think when they saw micah and Me together.

"I didn't mention it since I didn't see it as a big deal, Mom. It doesn't factor into the importance of why I'm with her. Does it matter really?"

"Have you ever been in an interracial relationship, Richard?"

Was My mother going to turn this into a "We Are the World" moment? Honestly, I could do without the lectures. At thirty-seven, I had many years of motherly advice to fall back on. A vault of advice to last Me a lifetime. I wanted more than anything for this conversation to end.

"No, Mom. I've dated a few women of color but nothing long-term."

My mother once again raised her brow to stare at Me intensely before looking away. She removed her oven mitts and walked over to the spice rack, sifting through the bottles. I'm pretty sure she could see through My bullshit.

"Hmm, well, first things first: 'sleeping with' and dating' are two different things, Rick. You know it and I know it. I wasn't always a mom, you know? I did date before your father."

Why the hell was she sharing this info? I hoped to God there was a point. I really didn't want to know that My mother had a sex life outside of My father. There's some shit I'd like to be ignorant of and that bit of information was definitely at the top of the list. She found the bottle she was searching for: cinnamon.

She placed it on the counter and continued to speak. "You know I've never been one to mince words, and I say this because I love you and you're my baby, but as progressive as the world is, not everyone will see what you and Micah have as beautiful. If you're not ready to face the hardships you might encounter because you two are together then you need to walk away now. It's 2009, everybody is so avant-garde because we have a black President, blah blah blah."

Oh boy.

"Sure, we live in New York City, but the majority of America is not like the city. You flew by the seat of your pants by having her move in with you. I'm sure you have your reasons why things have happened so quickly with you two, but honey, you should also be sure she's with you for the right reasons."

Well, tell Me how you really feel, Mom. What the hell was it with everybody second-guessing My ability to be in a serious relationship with micah? First Josh, and now My mother. My own *mother.* I began loosening the knot in My tie. For some reason, the temperature in the kitchen seemed to suddenly rise.

"Meaning what, Mom? If I'm supposed to be reading between the lines here, it sounds like you think she's with Me because of My trust."

"You said it, I didn't. But I hope you know whether or not she's interested in you for your money. I don't say this to be hurtful, sweetheart, but protect your assets. Your father and I raised you and Todd to use your intuition and good old-fashioned common sense. Our family is in a good place now because I made business decisions that incorporated both my head and my heart. I used them equally and never let one overrule the other."

I took a moment before responding to all My mother unloaded. Slow and deep breathing helped. What could I say about My mother? Lena was as genuine as they came. I appreciated her honesty, but I really didn't feel like hearing this shit on Thanksgiving of all days. Here I was thanking the universe for bringing such a lovely and charismatic woman into My life, and now I had to defend My relationship to My mother, of all people. Not to mention, she alluded that micah might be some kind of gold digger. My pretty girl hadn't known about My background until I chose to divulge the information.

"Rick, honey, calm down. I can tell by the way you're flaring your nostrils like a bull that you're upset. Let me backtrack a bit so you can see my perspective."

Leaning against the sink, I fully undid My tie and crossed My arms over My chest. A defensive stance for sure, but whatever, I was no longer feeling pleasant. "I'm listening, Mom. Go ahead."

After sprinkling a bit of cinnamon on the pies, she washed and dried her hands before pulling down a stack of dessert plates and coffee cups from the cabinet. After gathering spoons from the drawer, she said, "I don't know if Micah is with you for money, prestige, or because she genuinely cares about you. However, I have a feeling it's the latter. Richard, you know I'm brutally honest. Don't be upset at me for pointing out the obvious. Women go after men of means. I'm not saying that's Micah's motive, nor do I believe it, but I wouldn't be a very good mother if I didn't at least mention it.

"Honey, since Samantha, you've never spoken of any woman you were seeing or brought anyone to meet your father and me until today. Sam was the last woman we were privy to, then suddenly we get a call a few days ago that you're bringing your live-in girlfriend—whom we've never met—to Thanksgiving dinner. That was a shocker for us."

Well, there was a lot of truth there. My mother had kept asking what time I'd be over for dinner and I'd forgotten to follow up. By the time I remembered, I casually mentioned I'd be bringing micah. My parents hadn't known I'd been seeing anyone, let alone that she was living with Me.

"I knew it had to be serious from that declaration alone. I know Samantha meant a great deal to you and she seemed to have hurt you bad. So bad that you closed your heart off to love and happiness. I've been worried about you, kiddo. Your father constantly complained and wondered if we'd ever get the chance to be grandparents again. From what I've seen this evening, Micah has opened your eyes and your heart. I can see how much you care for her; it's written all over your face. You're different around her. Based on first impressions, I like her a lot, Rick, and your dad does as well. He told me so just before he helped bring out the turkey.

"I'm sure if I could pry him and Todd away from the television long enough, they'd contribute to this conversation.

"I don't care that Micah is black. What matters to me—to us—is that since you're moving this fast, it's for the right reasons. I want to know that she feels as strongly about you as you apparently feel about her. If you love her, then I wish you the best of luck, sweetheart. As I said before, if this leads to something more serious down the line, you'll have children, and although the makeup of the country is changing, some people still frown on interracial relationships and the offspring that come from those unions."

It was funny because I hadn't ever really given much thought to having children until micah. It had been a lingering thought, for sure, but with micah it was something I thought about all the time. To be honest, I often daydreamed about what our children would look like. Would they have her brown eyes or button nose?

"I'm not telling you anything you don't already know, but it just needs to be said. Your father and I don't care about any of it as long as you're happy. Caleb and William are getting too big to give me kisses without me having to twist their arm. I'm anxious to hear the pitter-patter of little feet around here again. I take my duties as Grandma seriously, you know."

I walked over to My mother and hugged her. Sure, she was verbose as hell, but I loved her. The old bird *was* brutally honest, but I knew she only had My best interests in mind. She always did.

"Mom, I'm pretty sure I love her. No. I know it. I love her and I do want to marry her someday. micah knows about the trust but only after I chose to reveal that information, and she doesn't care about the money. For a minute, she actually thought I was involved in illegal activity," I said, chuckling.

My mother squeezed Me around the waist. "Good to know that's not lingering over your relationship like a dark cloud. I know how you feel about the trust, but I have no regrets. I wanted my boys well cared for. But enough about that. She's got you talking about marriage, huh? Oh sweetie, you've got it bad."

I laughed. "I do, Mom. I fell for her pretty hard."

"Does she know how you feel about her?"

"No. Well, yes and no. I haven't told her that I love her but she knows that I care about her. My lack of telling her I love her has been a point of contention in our relationship. We actually had a bit of a blowup before coming over tonight."

"The woman picks up her life to move in with you and you haven't told her you love her? She must really have faith in you. You're my son, but that's questionable behavior, Richard. I'd haul ass if a guy I had moved in with hadn't told me he loved me."

"she does have faith in Me, and it humbles Me that she trusts Me so much, Mom. I don't know what I'm waiting on. I keep telling Myself that I'm waiting for the right time, but is there really such a thing as the right time? I guess I've just been scared to pull the trigger, but there's no reason for Me to continue to wait." As much as I didn't like having this conversation with My mother, it helped Me realize a few things. "I think it's about time I stepped up to the plate. Thanks for helping Me confront some thoughts I've been avoiding. I'll tell micah how I feel tonight when we're back at the condo. It's time."

"Some words of advice, sweetheart: If you can't see your life without her, if she's your first and your last thought and you'd be lost without her, that's as strong a feeling as any. Don't waste another minute not letting her know."

"Thanks, Mom, I appreciate the advice. I'm pretty rusty with this laying-My-feelings-on-the-line thing."

"Don't let your past hinder your future with Micah. If she's the one your heart beats for, tell her."

After I kissed My mom on her forehead and gave her a bear hug to end all hugs, I helped bring the dessert plates and coffee mugs out to the dining room and rejoined the rest of the family. There would be pumpkin pie and lovemaking in My immediate future. I was going to show My pretty girl how much I cared for her.

micah

Dinner with Rick's family was just the distraction i needed.

i was still angry, but the more time i spent with my Master's family, the more at ease i became. Conversation was warm and engaging. Dinner was delicious. Lena was a fabulous cook; i probably gained at least five pounds in one sitting.

Throughout dinner, my Master linked our hands together under the table. This gesture only intensified my anger. We were in front of His family, so i put on an Oscar-worthy performance. Every time i'd look to Him for answers, He simply smiled at me. i didn't want to smile—i was angry, damnit. Whenever He focused those baby blues on me, though, i couldn't help but return His smile. His bright eyes, combined with His grin, were my Kryptonite. Well, aside from the occasional ill-timed orgasm.

Seeing Rick's baby pictures and hearing stories about what my Sir was like as a kid induced much-needed chuckles. He was clearly embarrassed, but He took it all in stride, albeit with a flushed face.

i enjoyed getting to know my Master's family. They were lovely, kind, and fun. His father was such a flirt, which i found to be comical. Looking at my Master's dad was a clear indicator that He'd grow to be even more handsome as age settled in.

Overall, His family was very warm and welcoming, and His nephews were hilarious. Spending time with them reminded me of how much i missed my family. i'd see them for Christmas, but i longed for a hug from my mom. There was nothing like a mama's love.

Based on our phone conversations, my parents were anxious to meet Rick. Of course, they wanted to meet the Guy i had been living with the past few months. What parents wouldn't? my father had a ton of questions, and in not so many words, threatened to beat Rick's ass if He hurt his baby.

Being the youngest sometimes meant an overprotective father and brother hovering every time a guy showed interest in me. In my

Master's case, because things had ended awkwardly with Brent, my dad and brother wouldn't show Him mercy. i assured my daddy that Rick was good to me, but he wouldn't be satisfied until he could lay eyes on Him.

i had to mentally amend that last part of my previous statement. my Master had been good to me but we weren't in a good place, at least not on my end. He asked for time, but i wasn't particularly interested in giving it to Him.

When i had spoken to my parents about my relationship with Rick, they stated our racial difference didn't bother them, much, but of course my dad wished that i would end up with an upstanding black man.

you can't help whom you fall for.

i've dated all sorts of men, it just so happened that the last two men i'd been in relationships with were white. Just thinking of my dad sitting Rick down to give Him "the talk" had me on edge, and i still had a few weeks left until our voyage . . . if my Master still opted to go.

i wasn't sure what our future held at this stage.

Just as i was thinking of all the awful questions my brother, Darren, and our dad would toss at Rick, i was brought back to the moment at hand by my Master leaning into the cab and calling my name.

The door attendant named Stephen opened the vestibule door, ushering us inside our apartment building and out of the light late-November snow.

"Paul off for the holiday, I take it?" my Master inquired as we stepped into the lobby.

"Yes, Doctor Thomas. He and his wife went to visit their kids in Minnesota for the holiday."

"That's nice, sounds like a fun plan. Sorry you're working tonight, Stephen, but I hope you're able to salvage your Thanksgiving."

"Thank you, Doctor Thomas, I will try my best. You and Ms. Foster please do the same."

i smiled at Stephen and wished him a Happy Thanksgiving before my Master escorted me to the elevators, His hand resting at the small of my back. He pressed the button, and the doors parted, allowing me to enter. He followed closely behind, then pressed the button for our floor. His sparkling eyes quickly met my gaze as the doors closed.

Leaning against the elevator panels, He asked, "Glad to be home?"

"Yes, Sir," i replied, staring down at my heels. i didn't want to look at Him. It was difficult to be angry when He looked at me with such adoration.

"Did you enjoy yourself, micah?"

"i did, Master. Thank You for the evening."

"It was a pleasure to have you escort Me to dinner. My family seems to be taken with you, My mother especially."

"i enjoyed her as well. Everyone was very kind, Sir," i replied quietly.

Despite the wonderful time we had at dinner, there was still an elephant in the room. i couldn't give Him time. i was experiencing an eerie sense of déjà vu.

Earlier in our relationship, my Master said that our busy work schedules could put distance between us and He didn't want that to occur, so He asked that i move in with Him. We'd been living together for a some time now, and although there were still some scheduling issues, i didn't fully attribute our lack of penetrative sex to our schedules.

We'd done everything else, so i couldn't understand what the problem was. At first, i figured that the sexual distance might be due to the hours we kept, but since we were still having oral sex, that theory went out the window.

i'd been on the Pill for some time, but He was content with cunnilingus. It had never gotten anyone pregnant.

i just didn't understand. Why ask me to move in? Why did He say He wanted access to me at all times if He wasn't going to fully take advantage? Was this Brent Part Two?

The elevator chimed and the doors parted. Rick allowed me to exit the elevator ahead of Him. i stepped out into the hall and waited for my Master to lead the way to our apartment. He unlocked the door and ushered me into our dwelling.

Once i entered, i kneeled and awaited further instructions. Despite my simmering anger, i would not break protocol.

He whispered softly as He closed and locked the door behind Him, "micah, stand up."

i did what i had been trained to do. Every day, i greeted my Master this way. For the life of me, i couldn't understand why He didn't want me to present this way now. Was He also upset about earlier?

Nervousness and paranoia started to settle in as i rose to my feet.

my Master must have noticed my uneasiness, but instead of a look of sympathy, He scrutinized me. So He was still upset . . .

"Give Me your coat."

i removed my coat and handed it to Him as requested.

He hung up both our coats and quietly closed the closet door. When He was finished, He leaned against the door, and stared at me.

i quickly dropped my gaze and kept my eyes trained on the floor. It was the safest thing for me to do.

If i looked at Him, i was sure my resolve would break. The sight of His face was too much. my Master slowly made His way toward me, gently tilting my chin upward so that i was forced to look at Him.

"I need to ask: Were you being completely truthful when you said you enjoyed yourself tonight?"

i nodded. He stood so close, so incredibly close, and creased His brows together at my lack of verbal response.

"i'm sorry, Sir. To answer Your question, yes, i was being truthful. Tonight was wonderful and Your family is great. i really enjoyed meeting Your parents. Everyone made me feel very welcome, but Your mom went the extra mile and i appreciate it. No pun intended, but i was a bundle of nerves, especially after the egg was activated."

"I'm glad you had a good time. As for the egg, it was an amazing experience to watch you come without anyone the wiser. you made My dick hard. It was difficult for Me to maintain My composure as well. you're very sexy in the moment just before you're about to release."

i hated that He was talking about being turned on. i hated that He said i was sexy just before i came. i didn't want to hear any of this, so i stood before Him lightly brushing my hands over my dress as a distraction. i didn't want to focus on what He'd said.

If i focused too intently on His words i'd become flustered. Even when angry, He always had that effect on me.

"i'm glad You were entertained and aroused, Master. i really did make an effort to try to withstand the pleasure."

"Oh, I believe you. But. . . my imagination isn't exactly reliable tonight. How about you help Me out, micah? Tell Me, how wet are your panties?"

Shit.

"Uh . . . um. i'm not sure how to answer that, Sir," i replied, glancing away.

"Well," He said, "I know you may still be upset with Me, but your pussy adores Me. Since you're at a loss for words and My imagination is unreliable, give Me your panties, micah."

i continued to avert my eyes as i removed my underwear to oblige His request. i placed my saturated undergarment into His outstretched hand.

He sniffed them.

"micah, you drive Me crazy, so fucking crazy, pretty girl."

He placed my panties into His pants pocket before grasping my face in His hands.

i found it hard to believe that He would continue with our evening as if there wasn't an issue. i didn't like the way i felt. i was hurt, and dinner only temporarily took the focus off that pain.

"micah, look at Me, please."

i did as instructed and looked up to meet His gaze as a single tear fell from my eye. i couldn't hold it in any longer. i tried, but i couldn't do it anymore.

He wiped away my tear with the pad of His thumb. "I know you're upset with Me and you're hurting. I see it. I feel it.

"I feel your hurt, pretty girl, and I want to make it better. I swear to you I'm going to make it better. Tonight, may we do something different, micah?"

i wasn't sure where He was going with this, but i nodded before softly replying, "Yes. Yes we can, Sir."

"For the rest of the evening, no more formalities. You're Micah and I'm Rick. No more titles, no more roles, it's just you and me. You've been vulnerable throughout our entire relationship by submitting to me, and I'm going to even the playing field. You deserve my full loyalty as well."

I wasn't sure how to respond to what he just said, but the tears came faster. I didn't want to cry but I couldn't help it. Damn tears.

"I-I'm not sure I understand what you mean, Si—Rick," I managed to say.

"Micah? Would you please do me the honor of stripping bare and meeting me in the playroom in five minutes?" He asked, releasing me from his grasp.

I was confused. What was going on, and why did he want me to call him "Rick"? What did he mean by "even the playing field" and "full loyalty"? I had so many questions but no answers.

"Please, do this for me, Micah? Know that you've done nothing wrong; as a matter of fact, you've done everything right. Five minutes in the playroom, pretty girl? I promise to explain it all."

For now, I would oblige his request until we were in the playroom.

"Five minutes," I whispered as I turned and made my way to our bedroom to slip out of my clothing.

I don't think I'd ever heard such kindness and softness from Rick. I wondered what the change was attributed to. In the span of a few moments, he seemed different.

"Oh, and Micah?"

"Yes . . . Rick?" I replied, looking over my shoulder.

"Remove your egg."

I stood naked, admiring the snowfall through the panoramic windows. Despite the chaos below, the snow created a peaceful, picturesque scene, which was the polar opposite of what I was feeling at the moment. I leaned forward against the glass paneling, my nipples hardening on contact.

I think I felt his presence before I actually heard him enter the room. He approached me from behind, pressing his muscled frame against my back. His heat immediately warmed my body. He nuzzled against my neck and roamed his hands over my breasts and along my midsection. He began a sensuous assault that started with light nibbling on my ear and ended with his hand wrapped around my throat as he planted slow and deliberate kisses along my shoulders.

A moan escaped my mouth as I leaned back into his embrace.

When he turned me around to face him and our gazes finally met, I could detect something different in his eyes. I hadn't the slightest clue what exactly was different, but I felt it.

Without an exchange of words, he took hold of my waist and leaned down to kiss me. Our tongues met, and it was as if we were kissing for the very first time. It was tentative but telling. He was fully taking over all of my senses—so much so, I forgot to breathe. Asthma be damned. Everything about his kiss and his touch was different.

Rick was very deliberate with the gentle strokes of his tongue. His tongue moved with mine in perfect sync as he alternated between suckling my bottom lip and delivering sweet pecks to my face. It was a tender, soul-wrenching, curl-your-toes kind of kiss.

"Rick," I moaned. It felt unusual, hearing his name roll off my tongue.

He halted the kiss and took a deep breath, rubbing his forehead against mine. Despite the dimness of the room, when I looked up to meet his eyes, they shone brightly. The color had taken on a slightly lighter blue than I was used to seeing. I stood fascinated.

"Micah, I love you," He whispered.

I shook my head. This wasn't real.

I was pretty sure a gasp escaped my lips. I was hearing things. There was no way Rick said what I thought he'd said. "W-what?"

"I love you."

I was stunned into silence, still trying to figure out what was happening.

When I didn't respond, he hesitated a moment before continuing with his declaration. "I think on some level I knew I loved you the moment I laid eyes on you. It was the scariest feeling I've ever had in my life."

He let out an uneasy chuckle, his breath warm against my face as he spoke. "I've had many relationships, but nothing like what we have."

He hugged me tighter. "You wanted to know why I haven't made love to you yet, that's why. I waited so long to say that. I-I just didn't want to scare you away, Micah. I never wanted to only have sex with you. I told you from the beginning—I want everything."

I clasped my arms tighter around Rick's neck and let my tears flow freely.

He loved me.

Rick Thomas loved *me*.

This *was* real, and He felt the same way I had been feeling from the very beginning.

I stood on my tiptoes, leaning in to kiss him. "I love you, too, and I swear I'm not just saying that, Rick. I've felt the same way for some time but wanted proof that I wasn't alone in my feelings."

In a swift motion, he lifted me up from the floor and pressed me against the glass.

My legs wrapped around his waist and I anchored my ankles behind his back, my pebbled nipples brushing against his bare chest.

"You love me?" he asked, pushing a wayward lock of curly hair away from my face.

I nodded. "I do, very much."

"Tell me again."

"I love you, Rick," I whispered.

He latched his mouth onto my shoulder, licking and suckling his way down to my breasts. Oh God, his mouth felt like heaven.

Neither of us could catch our breath as Rick moved from one breast to the other, then kissed a path up my neck and collarbone before finding my lips again.

He broke the kiss, and I groaned in complaint. "Micah, sweetheart, please forgive me. I've waited too long for this, for you. I promise to make it up to you all night long, baby, I promise," he murmured in my ear, slipping his hand between our bodies and running his fingers lightly over my clit.

I whimpered when he thrust into me, my back bouncing off the window as Rick worked to release months of pent-up aggression. The dimly lit room and privacy glass prevented residents of adjoining high-rises witnessing me getting a pounding for the gods. The reflection of the city's lights twinkled in Rick's eyes as sweat trickled down his brow.

Rick fucked me like a man on a mission. He delivered sweet blow after torturous blow, and my pussy welcomed him home.

"You feel so fucking good, Micah. So good," he mumbled, glancing down between our bodies to watch his dick move in and out of me. He grunted in my ear and squeezed my ass. "God, you're so tight and so wet and fuck, Micah. Fuck, you feel incredible."

My breasts pressed against his muscled chest and my arms gripped him tightly around his neck, not ever wanting to let go. I never wanted this moment to end.

"Rick, mmm shit . . . that feels so good. Mmm . . . please don't stop."

"Always . . . I want this always. I've waited so long . . . you . . . feels so fucking amazing. Need just you, Micah, always." He ground out his words in between deep, powerful thrusts.

Nothing on earth could ever feel as good as I felt in this moment, but I wanted more.

He continued his wicked assault and fucked me like a man possessed.

I was certain I'd be unable to walk properly tomorrow—hell, probably not for a few days—but I willingly accepted the consequences.

He once again reached between our bodies and frantically rubbed my clit. "Come for me, Micah. Come on, let me hear how good this dick feels, baby."

That was all the encouragement I needed. Between his request and the way his dick was hitting my G-spot, there was no ability to resist. I didn't want to. Once the pad of his thumb made quick strokes across my clit, I felt myself unravel. "I'm coming. Oh God . . . I'm coming," I screamed. And cum I did.

My orgasm swept through me like a goddamn riptide, releasing so much sexual frustration. I orgasmed when we had oral sex, but this—this was different, so incredibly different. This was a connection of souls.

What Rick and I had exceeded love. It was more than body parts fitting together, more than just another sex act. He literally and figuratively plugged into me.

Rick picked up his pace. "Tell me you're mine, Micah. Tell me you'll always be mine."

"Oh, God. Yes . . . yes, I'm yours, my pussy is yours."

His thrusts became more forceful. My back and ass bounced off the window as he moved inside me.

"Almost there, sweetheart. Be mine. All mine. Can I come inside, baby?"

"Yes . . . you'll be the first—the only," I said breathlessly.

"It's just you and me, Micah. Erasing our pasts, starting fresh, baby. Forever and always."

"You're the only one to ever fill me up, Rick—mind, body, and soul."

He looked up from between our sweat-saturated bodies before kissing me with such intensity I thought he'd suck every last bit of oxygen from my lungs.

He grabbed a fistful of my hair, yanking my head back while slamming into me. "I love you, Micah. I love you, baby," he said as his warm cum flooded my channel. Rick stopped moving for a moment but he didn't put me down, nor did he withdraw from me. Instead, he rocked our bodies, softly rubbing his forehead against mine, staring into my soul.

It took few moments for our breathing to return to normal.

"Shit, I'm sorry. Did I hurt you, sweetheart? I didn't mean to be so aggressive. Are you okay?"

I nodded and delivered a sly grin. "Yes. I'm okay, and no you didn't hurt me. I'm sure I'll feel it tomorrow, but it was well worth it."

He laughed. "Give me ten minutes and I'll be ready for round two."

I smiled and ran my hands up and down his chest, savoring the feel of his pulsating heartbeat against my palm.

"I love you, Rick," I whispered, needing to say it again. I needed to know this wasn't a dream.

He peppered kisses all along my neck and jaw before saving the most tender ones for my lips.

"No one has ever come inside you before?" he asked as he slowly withdrew from me.

"No, not ever," I whispered, as his cum trickled down the inside of my thigh.

"Thank you, Micah. I'm honored," he replied, setting me down on the floor and leading me toward our bedroom.

I lay on my back as Rick moved in and out of my pussy at an excruciatingly slow pace. With our fingers intertwined, he buried himself deep inside me, with my legs firmly wrapped around his muscular ass, pulling him deeper.

Tears streamed down my face and he kissed each one of them away, making me feel so very cherished.

"I love you, Micah, more than anything in this world." He slowly glided his tongue across my lips and I obediently parted them, allowing him to explore. He broke the kiss to look into my eyes. "Thank you for giving me all of you, baby."

My heart had never been so full. I had been in a series of relationships over the years, but I had uttered the words "I love you" to exactly two lovers: Brent and Rick. One was history, and I was making history with the other.

I swore to myself that I would never let a man come inside me unless he was my husband, but I broke that vow and would likely break it a few more times before the night ended. It was an act I'd been saving for marriage. I'm old-fashioned that way, but I didn't regret letting it happen with Rick. Somehow, it felt right. Everything about being with him felt right. I'd been on the Pill for a few months, so there was no concern about me getting pregnant, but if that were to happen, I think Rick would be okay with it. We hadn't spoken of children in great detail, but he knew I had a strong desire to be a wife and mother someday, so what happened between us was indeed a very big deal.

After my hesitancy to move in with him without a more permanent commitment, Rick had assured me that collaring and marriage were also his end goals.

We never took things slow. Everything about our relationship was unconventional. It didn't matter much to us when certain milestones should occur—we did what felt right for us. But I still worried.

Up until an hour ago, I hadn't known how deeply Rick cared about me. How serious had he been about marriage? He knew my feelings and said he wanted the same things, but how truthful was that? He loved me all this time and never told me.

I was just as guilty, but I wasn't the leader in this union. His hesitancy to share his feelings made me feel skeptical, but I hoped that ultimately, what was happening tonight would change the scope of our relationship. He said it would, and I had to believe it was the truth.

I ceased thinking of what would come next and focused on enjoying the here and now and the sounds of our bodies meeting and my moans mingling with his grunts. With each deep stroke, his balls slapped against my pussy. I was experiencing sensory overload, and it felt amazing.

"Micah, fuck, your cum is all over me. Come on, one more time, baby . . . I want to feel you cream all over my cock."

One more time? Rick had already brought me to climax five times, and I was barely functioning. Multiple orgasms were exhausting. Rick wore me out, but I loved every minute of it.

Our coupling was the perfect illustration of a Dom/sub relationship. It was give and take, but when you fed off one another and an intense connection was established, it was some mighty powerful shit. Mighty powerful.

"Uhh . . ." was all I was able to get out before Rick crushed my mouth and swallowed my cries. The intensity of my orgasm made me feel as if I were on the verge of blacking out. It was that damn good. A few moments later, he followed suit, reaching his climax and spilled inside me.

To be with my man, my love, my Master in this manner, was wonderful and well worth the wait.

Rick was a phenomenal lover. I hadn't had very many sexual partners, but he stood out from the rest. He was extremely attentive and cared about my pleasure before his own.

After planting a slew of kisses along my breasts, he withdrew from me, rolled out of bed, and headed for the master bath. Silence followed, but words weren't needed. I heard water running before he returned a short time later with a damp washcloth in hand. Kneeling on the bed, he spread my legs wide, softly wiping away the visible remains of our lovemaking from my body. Rick sat back on his haunches and my gaze landed on his muscular thighs. He smiled down at me before bending to deliver the most loving kiss.

"Are you happy, Micah?"

"Very. This feels right," I replied with a wide grin.

"It feels right because we're right together. All I ever want is to make you happy."

He did just that. My heart was full, and it was full of the purest love I had ever known.

Aftercare

her Master

micah sat in the passenger seat of the rental car tinkering with the GPS on the dashboard as we pulled into her parents' driveway. her parents resided in a quaint neighborhood. I found their Spanish-style two-story house charming. micah's parents clearly had a love of gardening; the landscaping around the property was exquisite.

We arrived in California two days before Christmas Eve. Was I nervous? Hell yes. This trip was more than just Me meeting micah's relatives. I also wanted to get her parents' blessing for her hand in marriage. I was ready to take our relationship to the next level.

After Thanksgiving, micah and I were fucking like bunnies. I took her on damn near every surface in the condo. There were a few places left in the apartment that were untarnished, but I could say for certain that I would never look at our dining room table the same way. micah brought out My animalistic tendencies. All it took was a certain gesture, a certain outfit, or her uttering certain phrases for Me to bend her over a surface and fuck her silly. Oftentimes, the most mundane shit would set Me off, like preparing My dinner, folding the laundry, disinfecting the playroom, or on her hands and knees scrubbing the kitchen floor—I couldn't keep My hands off her.

As an early Christmas gift to Me, My pretty girl pierced her nipples. I can't express how goddamn ecstatic I was when she unveiled them. Our contract stated that no body modifications would be made without prior permission, but micah knew nipple piercings would be something I'd enjoy. I was like a kid in a candy store. Nipple play would become increasingly more satisfying for us both once they healed. It would take a few months, but I could be gentle until then.

I shut off the engine and turned to micah as she continued to tinker with the GPS. My hand covered hers in a soothing gesture. I could tell she was nervous, although I wasn't sure why.

"Now, something is clearly bothering you, micah. you've been fiddling with that damn GPS for the past ten minutes. Care to tell Me what's wrong, sweetheart?"

"i'm nervous, Master."

"I can see that. Dare I ask what about?"

micah released a light sigh before responding, "Most of my family—not just my immediate family—will be here, and they're going to rake You over the coals."

I found her concern for My well-being endearing. "I'm a big boy, micah. I think I can take some ribbing and light intimidation tactics. I'm pretty secure in what we have and what I offer you. No one can question that."

"my dad will certainly question it, Sir. And Darren? He has two daughters he watches like a hawk, and they're only five and eight. my brother is a bit ridiculous with the overprotectiveness."

I removed My hand from micah's and laughed. she was genuinely concerned with how I'd fare with her family. From the pictures I had seen, her brother was built like a linebacker and could probably kick My ass to Texas and back, but I'd sure as hell give him a run for his money. I certainly was no slouch, and My intentions with micah were more than sincere. Hell, I wanted to make her My wife. It didn't get more sincere than that.

After many secret rendezvous with jewelers, I picked out a stunning, vintage-style, four-carat princess-cut ring with a platinum band. As soon as I saw the ring, it screamed micah. It was powerful, delicate, and made a statement, just like My pretty girl.

Presently, it sat in the trunk of our rental, hidden inside the backpack I used as a carry-on.

"micah, don't you think you may be overreacting?"

she laughed as if I had made the most absurd statement. "Sir, with all due respect, don't say i didn't warn You."

I quirked My brow. Really? Hmm . . . this was going to be interesting. As we exited the car, a statuesque dark-skinned woman opened the front door and headed down the driveway to greet us. I could see where micah got her figure and impeccable skin. her mother was the personification of a "brick house." She had curves for days, and if genetics were any indicator, My pretty girl would look like that in about twenty years. I displayed a wide grin that rivaled the Cheshire Cat's just thinking about it. Oh, the future was looking very bright.

The woman whom I'd guessed was micah's mom ran toward her with her arms outstretched. "My baby!" she squealed, squeezing My pretty girl mightily.

They hugged for what seemed like an eternity. When micah broke free of her mother's embrace, her face was streaked with tears. micah mentioned that she was a mama's girl. she had a very intense relationship with her mother; being so far away from her had occasionally taken its toll. I was pleased that she'd be able to spend Christmastime surrounded by people who loved her dearly, just as I did.

her father soon joined them for a group hug. I leaned awkwardly against the car, waiting for acknowledgment. I knew My pretty girl hadn't forgotten her manners, she was simply caught up in emotion. I let her deviation from protocol slide.

It finally dawned on her that I was standing next to the car waiting for an introduction.

"Oh my gosh! i'm so incredibly sorry. Where are my manners?" she said, wiping away her lingering tears. she removed herself from her parents' embrace to walk over to the car and grab My hand.

"Mama, Daddy, this is my Boyfriend, Rick. Rick, these are my parents, Pamela and Monroe Foster."

I extended My free hand out to her father first. He was shorter than I imagined. I estimated him to be about five-foot-nine. He was stocky and reminded Me of a shorter version of Carl Weathers.

"Mr. and Mrs. Foster, it's a pleasure to meet you."

her father harrumphed as he shook My hand. "Hmm, so you're the latest one that's got my daughter shacking up with you?"

"Daddy!" micah squealed.

"It's okay, micah. It's a pleasure to meet you, Mr. Foster. I can understand your wariness regarding your daughter living with Me, but I assure you, micah is well taken care of."

156

"It's not her being taken care of that concerns me. Micah can take care of herself. It's what . . ."

"Daddy, can we please make it out of the driveway before you start the interrogation?" micah responded with a pleading look in her eyes.

Well shit, I guess micah's warning had meaning after all.

"Don't mind my husband. Hi, Rick, it's a pleasure to finally meet you," her mother said, extending her hand in My direction. "Micah has told us a lot about you. Please call me Pamela."

I shook her hand vigorously. "It's a pleasure to meet you, Pamela. I can see where micah gets her attractiveness."

Her father shot daggers at Me while her mother smiled when I laid on the charm. It wasn't as if I were lying. micah's mother was quite lovely.

"Can we help you with your things?"

"No, it's okay. We were thinking of checking into the Westin for the next few days. We wanted to stop off here first to spend some quality time with you both," I replied.

"You'll do no such thing. We have plenty of guest rooms. Monroe, would you help Rick with their bags while I show Micah the improvements we've made to the guest rooms?"

"Sure, sweetie," her father said before giving Me what I could only decipher as the evil eye. I was supposed to win this guy over and ask for his blessing to marry his daughter? I had My work cut out for Me.

micah and I were settling into our seats in first class, on a red eye flight back to New York City after having spent a week in California. It was the day before New Year's Eve and we were excited to head back home to celebrate the holiday. I was going to miss the San Diego sunshine for sure. Warm weather was always a welcome change in December. My plan was to propose to micah as the clock struck midnight the following day. Hopefully, I'd make it back to New York in one piece. micah currently held a death grip on My left hand as she snuggled against My shoulder. Flying made My pretty girl anxious.

I comforted her as our fellow passengers made their way to their seats, although it didn't matter much since she still held a tight grip on My hand. "Hey, we'll be home before you know it, sweetheart. If you sleep the entire trip, we'll be landing in New York by the time you wake up."

"i know. i just get a little uptight, Sir. Obviously, i understand how gravity works, but six hours in the air? It freaks me out. i've flown quite a bit for work and i should be used to it by now, but it never gets much easier."

I unlinked My hand from micah's to pull the blanket over our bodies. she tucked her legs beneath her bottom and returned to her snuggling position against My arm.

"you're going to sleep now?"

"Yes, Master. Unless of course You need me for something," she replied, awaiting a response.

"No, I'm fine. Get your rest."

I put My arm around her and stroked her hair as she began to drift off. We were about to take off and it was a struggle to keep My eyes open. I would soon follow micah into slumber.

On our last day in San Diego, I had told micah I'd stick around to chat with her family while she and her sister-in-law took the kids out for ice cream. During the latter part of our trip, her father had somewhat warmed up to Me. He was less hostile after Christmas. Maybe Santa Claus had something to do with it, but I assumed it had more to do with seeing micah and I interacting. After dinner on Christmas evening, her father and I played game of one-on-one in her parent's backyard. Nothing brings men together like a game of basketball. Just before sleep completely claimed Me, a slight smirk crossed My lips as I thought back on the most nerve-wracking moment of My life.

micah's father, Monroe, took a seat next to his wife, Pamela, on the couch. Their son, Darren, sat to her left.

"So you wanted to talk to us, Rick?" Monroe inquired.

"Uh, yeah, I did." Crossing My hands and leaning forward in the armchair, I replied, "I want to thank you all for your hospitality and allowing Me to stay in your beautiful home these last few days. While micah and I have been here, I've been on the receiving end of some unfiltered thoughts. she warned Me that with so many members of her family visiting, it would be highly unlikely that people wouldn't speak their minds. I know you all care very much about micah and her well-being, and so do I. I also know that due to her previous relationship with Brent, you're very wary of her dating another white Guy."

Darren coughed.

"No sense in avoiding the obvious. No one has mentioned it outright, although there have been some offhanded comments made referring to our racial differences."

"Well, hey, I want to say that it doesn't matter, but it does, Rick," Darren replied. "You seem like a nice dude, a good dude, and you clearly care about my baby sister, but the last white guy she thought she would be with long-term had no interest in settling down with her. He lead her on. The time that Brent spent fucking with her head could've—"

"You watch your mouth, Darren," Pamela interrupted, lightly slapping his hand.

"Sorry, Mama," he replied, rolling his eyes. "Anyway, the time she spent waiting on Brent to get his act together was time she could've spent with the guy she was meant to be with, white or black. Would she have gone through the same thing if Brent had been black? Who knows, but what I do know is she sat pining over an asshole until it dawned on her that the relationship wasn't going anywhere. Was it due to her being black? Again, I don't know, but my sister is good enough to settle down with and I'm tired of seeing guys not do right by her."

Fan-fucking-tastic. The new Boyfriend always *loves* being compared to the ex.

"Even before Brent, her track record with white men hadn't been the best. Maybe that's why I'm skeptical. Micah is a good woman with a good heart, Rick. She has one funky-ass temper, but she's a caring soul. She balances all of it well and deserves someone who sees what a treasure she is. My sister is worthy of being treated like a queen."

"Darren Foster, you've got one more time to get foul-mouthed in my home . . ." Pamela warned.

I couldn't deny what Darren said. micah was indeed worthy of being treated like a queen. I treated her as such daily. she was My submissive, but that only made her more regal in My eyes. she was everything I thought a woman should be.

Darren looked sheepishly in his mother's direction as he began yet another apology. "Sorry, Mama."

He quickly turned his focus on Me, and the sheepishness disappeared in an instant. I was now the recipient of a death glare. "I agree with you, Darren. micah is quite the treasure. I see her as nothing less than a queen."

micah's father, Monroe, chimed in, giving Me a piece of his mind. The hits just didn't stop coming. "You know, Rick, I want to dislike you, but I can't find a damn thing about you not to like. You're successful, you're well-spoken and well-rounded, you can talk about football and never tire of my shots at your sorry-ass Cowboys. You can play one hell of a game of basketball, you get along well with my brood despite their not-so-PC thoughts, you come from a good and stable home, and most importantly, you treat my daughter like she's the center of your universe."

"she is the center of My universe, sir. I'll let the cheap shot about the Cowboys go for now," I replied, chuckling.

"Yeah, yeah, yeah, forget about those sorry-ass Cowboys, but I have to admit my son has some valid points. We want to say that race isn't an issue but in reality it is. I like you so far, but I need to know, are you in this for the long haul with Micah? Because if not, let her be. Let her go so that she can find the man who will love her the way she needs to be loved. Of course, I would prefer that Micah was with a man who looks like her daddy, but what I want doesn't matter. I like how you present yourself. You're very attentive when it comes to Micah."

Why the hell was I continuously on the receiving end of the race discussion? First My mother, and now My future father-in-law. I know I hadn't dated many women of color prior to micah, but this wasn't a game to Me, this was My life. I wanted to start a future with this woman—I didn't give a fuck if she was blue. I also didn't give a fuck about people who may disapprove of our relationship. It was 2009. 2009! And interracial relationships were still a point of discussion? Why? Better yet, who cared? I was never the type to do things to please others, and I wasn't about to start now.

I could tell they weren't going to make this easy. I had to sell Myself to micah's nearest and dearest. I had to make them understand that even something so small as having her away from me for extended periods hurt. she was the missing puzzle piece in My life. I didn't care about all of the other shit. I only want to be with her.

"I'm not the white Guy looking for a black-girl fix, if that's what you're concerned about, Darren. micah isn't the representation of a fetish to Me. My time with her is meaningful and based on mutual attraction and respect. I'm also nothing like Brent. I've never asked micah much about him, because, frankly, the guy before Me is irrelevant. All I knew was that his loss and his mistakes led to Me and her. There was no comparison. We weren't in the same league."

I looked over to micah's father, making sure he was able to see the sincerity in My eyes. "To address your concerns, Monroe, I value all that micah is. she's a spectacular woman. As cliché as it sounds, her race doesn't matter to Me. I can admit that before micah I hadn't dated many women of color. Actually, I hadn't dated any, if I'm going to be completely honest."

"Then why her? Why now?" Monroe inquired.

Valid question, and I couldn't fault him for asking. If it were My daughter, I'd probably ask the same thing.

"Because I took one look at her and I wanted to get to know her. It just so happens that Fate led Me to her in her time of need. micah's race was never part of the equation."

Darren cleared his throat. "Fate, hmph."

Her brother took every opportunity he could to bust My balls. I had to reel in My aggression because he wasn't just some average Joe challenging Me, he was My submissive's brother. I had to remember that winning his approval was the end goal.

"Do you love our little girl, Rick?" Pamela asked.

"I do, ma'am, with all My heart. I'd swear on a stack of Bibles in front of every damn priest imaginable if I felt it would make a difference. I do love micah, very much."

"And what are your intentions with her?"

Finally, My moment to shine. I was nervous but more concerned with micah's family seeing that I was the best choice—the only choice—for her. My love and dedication was incomparable. she was Mine. Standing up to reach into the pocket of My cargo shorts . . . I took a deep breath, cupping the black velvet box I'd been hiding for the past week in My sweaty palm.

"Well, that's why I wanted to meet with you all. micah and I have been living together for a few months. Our relationship has moved quickly, but it's at a pace we're both comfortable with. A love story can begin anywhere, and ours began the night I saved her life.

"My intentions, Pamela, include asking all three of you for your blessing. I'd like your permission to ask for micah's hand in marriage. I want to spend the rest of My life with your daughter," I replied, opening the box that held the gleaming diamond ring.

Darren whistled. "Shit, you give new meaning to go big or go home!"

"I told you to watch your mouth in my house, young man. I'm not going to say it anymore," Pamela reprimanded Darren, slapping him on the leg.

"Dangit, Mama, sorry," Darren replied, rubbing his leg. "That thing is huge!"

"You've made a beautiful choice, Rick. You have good taste," Pamela remarked. "The ring is absolutely, positively gorgeous."

I thought so too. It was hell trying to find the perfect ring, but it spoke to Me. There was no doubt about it, I had the best selection for My pretty girl.

"Thank you, Pamela," I replied nervously. Shit, would they just tell Me everything was okay? I needed to know that they wouldn't give Me any crap when I asked micah to marry Me. Regardless of what they said in this moment, I *was* going to ask her. I sought their permission as a courtesy, but even if they didn't give Me their blessing, it wouldn't deter Me. I asked out of respect for micah. I know she wanted her family to accept Me as Mine had accepted her.

"Do you promise to honor her, Rick, and always do right by her? That means even when you both are mad as hell with each other," Pamela inquired.

"Yes, ma'am. I swear it."

Pamela nodded at My declaration and Monroe chimed in, "You know if I say yes to this, Rick, I'm handing over my responsibilities to you. Not all of them, but the day-to-day stuff. As Micah's father, I can only do so much for her, but as the man in her life, you're responsible for a whole lot more. It becomes your job to see that she's happy and cared for. It becomes your primary responsibility to be there for her when she's hurt and in need of affection and protection. If you bring children into the world, your love for her expands. Asking my daughter to be your wife is something that will change you both. Don't ask for our blessing unless you're absolutely sure."

It sounded like I was going to get a thumbs up. I hoped everyone was on board, but I was still unsure where everyone stood.

"I'm absolutely sure, Monroe. In all My thirty-seven years on this earth, I've never been more certain about anything in My life."

"Well then, you have my blessing," he said, standing to shake My hand. "That's one hell of a rock you got for my baby girl."

Goddamnit, her father gave Me a yes. I was feeling mighty high. Fathers are usually the toughest people to win over, but he said yes. I'll be damned, he said yes.

"Thank you so much for your blessing, Monroe. micah deserves the best, sir."

Pamela walked over to Me and stood on her tip toes to kiss My cheek. "As long as you put many smiles on her face every day, you have my blessing, sweetheart. Be good to my girl, Rick."

"Thank you, Pamela. I promise to do just that," I said, beaming.

A unanimous yes from the parents. One left to go.

Darren reluctantly stood up from the sofa and looked at Me. He was maybe an inch shorter than Me, but if I didn't know any better, I'd think he played pro ball. The guy was solid and staring daggers at Me. He walked over and extended his hand before breaking into a smile. "As long you're not playing some jungle-fever shit, you have my blessing. But if you hurt her, I know where you live and I'll make your life hell."

"Darren! What did I say? You watch your mouth!" Pamela squealed.

I laughed and pulled him into a bro hug. "Thanks, man. This means a lot. No need to make My life hell. I promise to do right by your sister."

"So when do you intend to pop the question?" Monroe asked.

"New Year's Eve. So you can understand why I needed your blessing sooner rather than later."

"Understood. Well, good luck to you, and call us after," Monroe responded.

"I will. You have My word."

my Master and i spent the entire day doing something i would've never suspected He would take an interest in. We landed in New York City after an overnight flight and spent a few hours sleeping in. When we awoke, we had a midmorning fuck-a-thon, a shower, and a light snack, then Rick asked me what i'd like to do for the remainder of the afternoon.

For the longest time, i'd been wanting to go to Barcade, but kisa and i could never manage to sync our schedules and make the trip to Brooklyn, so i suggested my Master and i go instead.

Barcade, a microbrewery in the Williamsburg section of Brooklyn, featured vintage arcade games and a variety of tasty beers. We hopped on the subway, which was a feat in itself, since my Master was never one to utilize mass transit. Once we made it to Brooklyn, He indulged His silly side and gave me a piggyback ride in the partially melted snow from the train station to our destination.

Riding on Him those few blocks, i laughed so hard my sides ached. He threatened to drop me more than a few times before we made it the brewery, but i knew He would never make good on His threat. i was seeing a side of my Master i hadn't been privy to. He was lighthearted and, dare i say, fun. Not to make it seem like Sir was a stick in the mud, but He was much more into partaking in cultural activities like the opera and ballet as opposed to the more mundane aspects of New York City nightlife. He wasn't much for bar-type atmospheres. Don't get me wrong, my Master would let loose whenever an opportunity presented itself, but rarely did i get to see Him in such a whimsical mood. He'd been more carefree in the past two days. i wondered what brought on the change, but i was pretty sure the Cali sunshine had something to do with it. It had that effect on people.

We arrived at Barcade and started with a few games of pinball followed by air hockey, and concluded with intense battle rounds of Ms. Pac-Man and Centipede. i'm very serious about my classic video games. We also drank a few beers and indulged in a basket of curly fries and burgers while reflecting on our holiday in Cali, since we both slept during most of the flight.

When we arrived back at our condo, it was close to seven o'clock. my Master informed me that He made plans for us for the evening and i had forty-five minutes to get ready. The clock was ticking. i wasn't informed as to what we would be doing, but i was told it would be a surprise i would never forget.

After showering, flat-ironing my hair in record time, and applying my makeup to perfection, i left the bathroom to select my dress choice for the evening. my options weren't easy. i had to choose from one of two dresses my Master had purchased for me as Christmas gifts. One was a stunning off-the-shoulder teal number. It fell just above my knee and had a split up the side that didn't leave much to the imagination. The other was longer and white with gold embellishments along the scoop-neck collar. It did wonders for my cleavage. i wondered if my Master had help picking out the dresses. my instincts told me no, since He had such impeccable taste, but i secretly wondered how He was so in tune with what was new and hip in women's attire. It was unusual yet mildly appealing.

i selected the white dress; i had the perfect pair of gold stilettos to complement it. To be honest, not only did i choose the white because of the cleavage incentive, but it looked great against my rich complexion. i was sure my Christmas gifts set my Master back a couple thousand dollars. i balked at the extravagance but He reprimanded me, stating that since it was a holiday, He wanted to be generous.

i humbly accepted His offerings without further comment.

Just as i was zipping myself into the dress, Sir entered our bedroom. He opted to get ready in the guest room so we'd be on time for our evening plans. i had a tendency to take quite a long while to get ready and was pretty sure He had enough of my bathroom hogging.

He approached me and then wrapped His arms around my waist, delivering one of His soul-stirring kisses that momentarily stripped me of breath.

"you look beautiful, micah. Stunning, actually," He said, slowly pulling away from me.

Despite the fact that my lips were no longer joined to His, His presence lingered like a phantom touch.

"I'm glad you selected the white dress. I have to be honest, I liked that one much better than the teal, although they're both flattering on your figure."

"Thank You, Master," i replied, bowing my head.

"Are you ready to go?"

"Yes, Sir, i need to grab my purse and i'm ready."

"Great, I'll meet you by the front door in five minutes," He replied, exiting our bedroom.

Once Rick left the bedroom, my stomach suddenly decided to do the wave. i was nervous and i immediately wanted to barf, but i wasn't about to spoil a dress that likely cost a grand. i was never a fan of New Year's Eve. It was one of those holidays that i'd much rather skip. People made such a big deal over a few moments in time. Who cared what happened at midnight? Unnecessary pressure was placed on couples to make the evening special. i would have preferred to stay at home snuggled on the couch with my Master in my pajamas, but He made plans for us and wanted to ensure that we rang in the New Year in style. He hadn't revealed what we would be doing. Whatever it was, i'm sure it wouldn't disappoint.

We stood outside of New York City Center and my Master fought through throngs of people to get us a cab. Trying to catch a cab a few blocks away from Times Square on New Year's Eve is next to impossible, but luck was on our side. We'd just exited the venue after watching a performance of Alvin Ailey American Dance Theater. i loved Ailey, and i was surprised when my Master informed me once we left our apartment that we would be spending the earlier part of our evening enjoying a performance before heading to a late dinner.

Despite the fact that it had snowed earlier in the week, most of it had melted. It was unseasonably warm in New York City for this time of year. i think we brought back some of the California sunshine. The weatherman said the high was fifty degrees, which is practically beach weather in late December.

We could have easily walked to our destination since the weather was so pleasant, but i was grateful that my Master thought ahead. i completely forgot about the sky-high stilettos i was wearing. Even if our destination was only a few blocks, i would be in a serious amount of pain by the time we arrived. Once we were situated inside the cab, He tenderly caressed my hand and linked His fingers with mine while instructing the cabbie to head to the Empire State Building. Traffic was a horrendous nightmare, but i was content just being with Him.

"Did you enjoy the performance, micah?"

i couldn't contain my smile even if i wanted to. "Yes, Sir, it was phenomenal. i had no idea You were interested in Ailey."

He lifted our joined hands to His lips and planted a soft kiss on the back of my hand.

"you underestimate Me so. I like variety of things, but I have a feeling you have Me pegged as some uptight asshole. I do let go, you know."

As much as i tried to stifle my laugh, i failed miserably, and a chuckle escaped my lips. He raised His brow, which i interpreted as Him wondering what i found amusing. Well, i didn't have to wait long for the confirmation.

"Wait a minute—you actually believe that I'm uptight?"

i wasn't sure how to respond to that so i sat quietly as my teeth grazed my lower lip.

"I'm waiting for your answer," He said, lifting my chin to meet His gaze.

i was hesitant to respond because the last thing i wanted to do was have my Master feel as if i were insulting Him, but He had always asked for honesty and open communication.

"Well, You're kind of a workaholic, Sir, and the only time i really see You let loose and relax is when we're in the playroom."

"I beg to differ, pretty girl—you see Me let loose *outside* the playroom too." His tone was dripping with sexual innuendo.

The pointed look He gave me ignited a searing heat between my thighs, causing me to shift my position. i knew exactly what He was referring to. The Man was turning me into an exhibitionist.

"In any case, I'm not uptight. I enjoy lots of things. I'm anxious to explore more, but I haven't had a partner to indulge with. Now that I have you, that will change."

"Of course, Sir," i whispered. He always had a knack for riling me up, but now wasn't the time to give in to my innermost desires.

After an incredibly long journey, which on a normal day would've been a five-to ten-minute cab ride, we arrived at our destination thirty minutes later. The driver pulled up to the Empire State Building; my Master paid the fare before helping me out of the cab. Linking my arm with my Master's, we made our way to the entrance of the building.

It never dawned on me that we'd be entering the Empire State Building. i assumed our plans would include dining at a nearby restaurant, but Sir planned for us to be inside the landmark building, although i had no idea how that would happen. It was after 10:30 p.m. on New Year's Eve. Of course, my curiosity was piqued.

"Sir, how will we make it inside? It's New Year's Eve, i think the building is closed, and . . ."

"Shh, pretty girl, I've got it covered and FYI, the building isn't closed, sweetheart. Normally, this place would be flooded with people wanting to get a glimpse of the city and watch the ball drop, but I've made special arrangements for the evening. It cost a pretty penny, but it was well worth it," He said as we approached two men who stood at the revolving doors.

"Doctor Thomas, it's a pleasure to have you here this evening," said the man at the door. "Everything has been prepared to your specifications. You can go on up."

"Thanks, Mike, much appreciated," my Master commented, directing me through the revolving doors.

What on earth was going on?

i stepped out of the elevator to behold one of the most spectacular sights i had ever witnessed. The room was, in a word, astonishing. my Master transformed the floor, which was one level below the observation deck, into a majestic vision. Beautiful bouquets of red and white roses were displayed. A path of rose petals guided us into the room while candlelight cast a soft glow all around.

A waiter dressed in a tuxedo stood next to an immaculately set table for two. kisa, dressed in a French maid uniform, sauntered past us to stand next to the waiter.

i did a double take to be sure she was really there.

"kisa? What the hell are you doing here?" i asked, my voice rising to an insane pitch. i was utterly confused.

she looked as if it were perfectly normal for her to be there. "i'm here to assist Theodore," she said while motioning toward the gentleman standing next to her, "and make your New Year's Eve memorable. We'll be your wait staff for the evening. Just relax and have fun, micah. Trust me," she said, winking.

What the hell was going on? i turned to my Master for answers and He simply smirked. Yep, something wicked this way comes.

"micah, I believe Theodore is waiting for you to be seated," He replied.

i turned back to the elegant table where our waiter stood patiently waiting for me.

This was going to be one interesting New Year's Eve dinner.

micah's engagement ring was burning a hole in My goddamn pocket. We'd just finished dinner, and I was a nervous wreck. It was a struggle to maintain a cool and calm demeanor.

micah didn't seem to think anything was amiss. i'm sure kisa would've said something if My behavior was a little off. After dinner, micah excused herself to use the ladies' room with kisa in tow.

My pretty girl was predictable. I knew she was fishing for the reason kisa was here tonight.

Including kisa in My proposal idea came to Me on our trip back from California. With micah's family being so far away, I knew once I proposed, My pretty girl would want to share the news with someone close to her. Since her family wasn't near, kisa was the next best thing.

Planning this night helped Me develop a newfound respect for kisa. Initially, she wasn't a fan of Mine, but I didn't take it personally. she was very protective of micah and wanted the best for her, a true sign of a genuine friend. they'd experienced their fair share of assholes, and, well, kisa was still experiencing them.

From what micah had confided in Me, kisa had been on a quest for a suitable Dom but continued to come up empty. I'd have to refer her to a few Friends. Although I had no clue what kisa was into, I could think of a few Guys to introduce her to. If nothing else, she'd at least get some decent playtime and have an experience she'd likely never forget.

The ladies returned from the restroom, and i signaled to kisa with a subtle look that it was showtime. I was certain, despite micah's numerous pleas, kisa didn't spill the beans about My plan for the evening.

I wanted tonight to be extra special. It's not every day You propose to Your submissive. When micah looked back on this night, I wanted her to remember perfection. I was never really a fan of New Year's Eve, but it symbolized a new beginning. People have a habit of making resolutions they never stick to, but I wanted to start My year off on the right foot. I wanted micah to know that I wanted to spend the rest of My life with her. That was sure to bring in good luck for a new year.

kisa got the hint and cleared the table. Theodore followed suit. As they worked to clean the table, My attention traveled to micah's cleavage.

Goddamn, I made a good choice with her dress selection. It looked as if it was molded to her body and the white looked remarkable on her complexion. Taking the last sip of her champagne, My sweetheart offered her empty glass to Theodore, who placed it onto the cart before he and kisa were on their way.

"Would you like dessert?"

she dabbed her mouth with her napkin before responding, "No, Sir. i couldn't possibly eat another bite."

"Hmm, not even chocolate-covered strawberries?" I teased.

she laughed. "No, not even chocolate-covered strawberries. But if we could take some home, that would be great, Sir."

"I can make that happen. I can even think of interesting ways to use the extra chocolate sauce."

micah, in a predictable move, cast her eyes on her hands, which were clasped in her lap. I found it amusing that whenever I taunted her with a sexual innuendo, she'd clam up. My pretty girl was a highly sexual being, which was such a goddamn turn-on, but I brought out her shyness as well, and it was adorable.

I never tired of ruffling her feathers. Despite all the dirty shit we had done and all the soft limits I had pushed, she still became embarrassed when I made naughty innuendos.

I had fucked her throat with unyielding force, yet she blushed at the mention of what I could do with chocolate sauce. Fucking adorable.

"Since we're here and we have this wonderful scenery, micah, let's take advantage of it and head up to the observation deck. We'll have the best view in the city as the ball drops." I glanced at My watch and noticed it was quickly approaching midnight. "We have about fifteen minutes."

micah nodded, indicating she was into the idea. "Sure, Sir, that sounds nice."

I stood up to help her out of her chair. Theodore and kisa appeared with our coats. As I assisted micah with putting on her coat, kisa winked and mouthed to Me, *Good luck*. Luck? I didn't want to sound too cocky, but I don't think I needed much luck. Sure, I was nervous, but I had a feeling that this would go smoothly.

We lived together, met each others families, and did everything else a couple tends to do. What else was left? Granted, our relationship progression was unconventional, but c'est la vie.

I think My paternal grandparents perfectly illustrated that time didn't matter much when the heart wants what it wants. My grandfather Jesse knew My grandmother for exactly two months before he proposed and they married. They were together for fifty-two years until My grandfather passed away during My sophomore year of high school. My grandmother passed a few weeks later. When you're with someone for that long, I think you likely die of a broken heart. The love of her life was gone and she couldn't continue without him.

I wanted that kind of love with micah. I wanted forever.

We climbed a few flights of stairs before we were greeted by the most awe-inspiring view. The wind whipped wildly as I held the door open for micah to step onto the observation deck. Although micah's hair was pinned back from her face, it blew in the wind. It was a sight to see her thick mane sway to and fro; she had straightened it for the evening. It was beautiful. she was beautiful. I'd never been more certain about anything in My life. This woman held the key to My heart, and I wanted to be with her always.

As micah took in the view, My palms became sweaty while watching her.

This is what I get for talking shit about not needing luck. I think kisa jinxed Me. What I wouldn't give for a shot of Jack Daniels right now. Although I was clearly a bundle of nerves, I was grateful for the excellent weather conditions. It seemed as if Mother Nature gave Me her blessing by providing Me with a clear and unobstructed view of Times Square and the island of Manhattan. Whatever direction we chose to look, twinkling lights surrounded us. It was pretty damn stunning. I loved My city.

I stood by the door of the observation deck for a moment longer, admiring micah before gripping her from behind. My arms wrapped around her waist as I snuggled against her body.

she leaned into My embrace.

Glancing at My watch, I noted the time—11:51. It was now or never.

I took micah's hand and walked toward the center of the observation deck as the wind whipped around us. Releasing her hand, I took a few deep breaths. Shit. I silently prayed I didn't fuck this up.

My sweetheart had her eyes trained on Me as I lowered Myself down on one knee.

This was the moment when I'd pour My heart out. I hoped she'd accept all I had to say. I'd never been this bare with anyone, but I couldn't let fear win. she was vulnerable for Me every single day; I could express vulnerability for a few minutes.

micah stared at Me with her mouth agape. It finally dawned on her what was about to take place, and tears came to her eyes. I didn't want to see her cry, but I knew they weren't tears of sadness.

I took her hand in Mine, and the words came naturally. "micah, some months ago, after what was probably one of the worst days I've ever experienced in My medical career, I went to Spanxxx seeking refuge. I was angry. I was bored. I was lonely. I needed a distraction and was hoping to blow off some steam with a little play. Instead, I was gifted with more than I could have bargained for.

"I wasn't looking to settle down; I could barely date. My work schedule was awful, not to mention, I wasn't interested in the women I met. No one held My attention but you. you walked in and it was like a magnet was pulling Me toward you. From the moment I laid eyes on you, I wanted to get to know you. My intention was to have a few words with you and take it from there, but things went so much further than I could've ever imagined.

"This is where I get new age-y," I said, letting out a slight chuckle as I glanced up at her tear-streaked face. "I know you're not much of a believer in Fate, but I am. I was at Spanxxx the night we met because I was supposed to be. I was meant to save you, micah. I love you and nothing in My life has ever felt as good as the love I have for you."

I released her hand and reached into My pocket, pulling out the box that held the ring. micah stood before me trembling. I'm not sure if it was from the cold or the wind, but I wanted to scoop her up and protect her from everything.

I opened the box to present the ring. The look on her face was worth every penny.

"micah marie foster, would you do Me the honor of becoming My wife and My submissive for life?"

Flashes of light brightened the sky as fireworks went off in the far distance. I supposed the ball had dropped, but it didn't matter. What did matter was that there was no instantaneous yes. There was silence, a silence that likely lasted mere seconds but seemed like an eternity to Me.

I was honest.

I was succinct.

I was waiting for an answer.

she bum-rushed me, almost knocking me to the ground.

"YES! Yes, Sir. Yes, yes, yes, i'll marry You!"

Well, damn. I smiled so hard My face hurt.

I placed the ring on micah's slender finger and admired how beautiful it looked.

she stared down at Me. "May i, Sir?" she asked.

I nodded. micah hiked up her dress and kneeled in front of Me. she was slightly below eye level due our height difference, but she leaned in and delivered a kiss that was honestly the sweetest thing I'd ever experienced. Oh, how the tables had turned.

"i will always kneel for You, Master, because i want to. Thank You for loving me the way i deserve to be loved."

Epilogue

Late Summer 2014

her Master

After I proposed to micah, we were married a few months later. Actually, we decided on a destination wedding, on what would mark nine months together.

We wed on a beach in the Bahamas in a small ceremony with limited family and very close friends.

A few weeks before our wedding, we had a collaring ceremony in our apartment. Mistress Sybil, Master Otho, Mistress Carlisle, Josh, kisa, and a few other friends in the scene came. It was also small and intimate, but, in My eyes, carried more importance.

My duties as a Master and a Husband overlapped; My foremost duty was to protect and guide micah through everything life chose to toss at us. For the rest of My days, I would lead and she would follow.

As part of our collaring ritual, micah and I tattooed each other's initials on the inner part of our ankles. Master Otho had many talents, and tattoo art was one. While everyone mingled after the ceremony, we snuck off to the playroom for our new ink.

As a token for micah to wear daily, I purchased a sterling silver T-bar closure chain necklace from Tiffany & Co. Only the best for My girl. Surely, a stainless steel collar would look a wee bit unusual at her place of employment, so the necklace was a wonderful substitute.

For My token, micah surprised Me with a Rolex. I hadn't expected something so extravagant. It didn't seem to be her style, but My sweetheart kept Me guessing, as always. micah had the words "Forever Your pretty girl, love, micah" etched onto the back. I've worn it with pride every day since.

Currently, I was watching micah, having just wrapped up a phone call with a colleague about a patient's diagnosis. My everything just came down the slide with our twenty-two-month-old daughter, Perry, in tow.

Perry laughed and giggled in her mother's arms. Every time I looked at her, I was amazed by the little person micah and I had created. Whenever I thought of her conception, My smile widened as memories played through My mind. That night I had received the best damn welcome home ever. We worked hard to create our bundle of animated joy.

My balls tightened at the thought.

Our Perry Elizabeth was beautiful. She inherited My light blue eyes, and they were stunning against her smooth, honey-brown complexion and wild, curly, brownish-blonde mane.

Genetics can surprise you. I never anticipated Perry would inherit My eye color. The blue darkened to blackish cobalt when she was upset, just like Mine, which happened often—like when micah and I refused to give her a cookie with her afternoon snack.

The day she was born, I stared at her tiny, wrinkly body and cried. I hadn't cried since I attended My grandfather's funeral. The closest I came was the day I saw micah walking down the aisle toward Me in her wedding dress. My eyes pooled with restrained tears—she looked like a princess. I was blessed.

I was never a very religious Man, but I was spiritual enough to realize that I'd been gifted with good fortune that brought a remarkable lady into My life.

Perry ran toward Me, her little arms flailing.

"Daaa-dee!" she screamed when I caught her and lifted her up.

"Hi, pumpkin," I replied, kissing her chubby cheek. Moments like this made Me cherish fatherhood the most. The littlest things could brighten My day.

micah walked over to us, greeting Me with a kiss on the lips. I noticed the frown upon her face; she was clearly upset.

"What's wrong, sweetheart?"

"Nausea, my Love. Coming down the slide with Perry brought on a major wave of queasiness. It came out of nowhere, and now, i feel like crap."

she had taken to addressing Me as "my Love" in front of Perry. While micah and I were very much fulfilled in our lifestyle, we thought it best to give Perry and our future children a sense of normalcy at home. We saved the formalities for when we were alone, thus, micah's submission was subtle when Perry was around.

What mommy and Daddy did behind closed doors was for us, and only us.

"Ready to head home?"

"I can make you some of that ginger tea you like. Maybe if you eat a few saltines, it might reduce the nausea."

Perry placed her head on My shoulder and put her tiny hands around My neck. "Daddy, I sweepy."

"We're leaving soon, pumpkin. Once mommy gives the okay, we can go. I'm sorry you're feeling ill, micah, but the timing is perfect. It's naptime for our little girl."

"Yes, my Love, i'm ready. i could really use some tea—anything to get rid of this feeling—and we can put Perry down for her nap. i don't have the energy to do much more than push the stroller. i forgot how awful this stage is."

micah's eleven weeks pregnant, to be exact. she didn't begin to display any symptoms of morning sickness until earlier this month. Call Me superstitious, but I had a strong feeling this time it would be a boy. My instincts tended to be on point when I had a feeling like this. micah's been very ill this time around. Surprisingly, her bouts of morning sickness were virtually nonexistent with Perry. I chalked it up to boys being more rambunctious. Sensible logic, no? Well, maybe it was simply wishful thinking, but I really wanted a son. Honestly, I didn't particularly care if we ended up with another girl, as long as our baby was healthy, but I found Myself thinking of a boy to carry on the Thomas name.

micah pushed Perry's stroller while I held our daughter in My arms, smelling of sunshine and baby powder, and of course Perry fell fast asleep en route to our condo.

Once Perry woke up from her nap, micah and I intended to take her to My parents' place. She'd be spending the weekend with them.

This weekend was about My pretty girl and I reconnecting. When there was a toddler running around, hardcore play wasn't happening.

For the past few weeks, My sex life had pretty much come to a standstill, and it was driving Me mad. Between micah's sickness and Perry needing our attention, My dick was weeping for mercy. Our playroom hadn't seen action in a little while, but we were going to remedy that tonight. I'd have to be a little more tender than usual since micah was with child.

My parents had agreed to take Perry one weekend a month while My pretty girl and I got reacquainted. Of course, they had no fucking clue what went on during that weekend. If they weren't available, Todd and Stephanie agreed to babysit. Perry loved to play with Caleb and William, and despite being much older, they humored her.

It wouldn't be so bad if My in-laws were closer and a part of the mix, but with micah's family living in Cali, it wasn't feasible. We were planning a trip to visit her parents next month, before she got further along in her pregnancy and flying was nixed.

My pretty girl missed her family. she utilized FaceTime and Skype so everyone was able to keep up with Perry and how quickly she was growing. My pumpkin loved being on camera. I found Myself laughing often when she would burst into "Twinkle Twinkle, Little Star" with micah's mother and father watching her intently. We haven't told them about micah's pregnancy yet; we wanted to share the news with them in person.

My little girl will be a big sister in a few months.

After walking a few blocks, we made it to our apartment building, and I looked over at micah as Paul held the door open for us to enter. she met My gaze, and I winked at her as we made our way toward the elevators. she walked ahead of Me, pushing the stroller, and My eyes were trained on her ass. In that moment, she was the sexiest fucking thing within a five-hundred-mile radius.

Maybe it was the fact that I knew life was blooming inside of her, a life that I put there. Fuck, that's hot. I couldn't wait to get her alone and bury Myself deep in her pussy.

Any stolen moments I got to spend alone with My pretty girl were heaven.

Most mornings, when I woke up before micah and Perry, I found Myself watching micah as she slept, amazed at how much time had passed.

Five years strong and we've done so much within that time. I was never one to truly believe in soul mates or love at first sight. Fuck that. After what happened with samantha, I kept any emotional attachment at bay. I could admit My emotional growth was stunted. It took Me a long while to reach a good place. Love wasn't something I was ready for because I wasn't open to it, but all it took was one night. One night and Fate led Me to her.

I saved her life, and she saved Me from a life of emptiness.

I love micah with all My heart and soul. Many kinksters were of the school of thought that because you had certain proclivities, you'd never meet someone who shared your same feelings. When you denied what turned you on, what you got was a string of bad dates and forgettable sex that never led to anything. Yep, I had known that pattern fairly well, and frankly, trying to blend into the vanilla world could be a pain in the ass.

I had spent a lot of time denying what I wanted after samantha left, believing My "deviant" interests prevented Me from finding someone who accepted Me as I was. Just when I was erecting a wall to shield Myself from developing any emotional connection with a woman, micah came into My life.

Timing was everything.

I came across a quote once, I had no idea who said it, but it went something like this: "The longer you wait for something, the more you appreciate it when you get it, because anything worth having is definitely worth waiting for."

Our paths were meant to cross that night at Spanxxx. micah and I were two people who wanted the same things in life. Just because we found kink and a D/s relationship more appealing, it didn't mean that we didn't dream of the house with the white picket fence—our house would just have a dungeon in the basement.

Our love story was unconventional, to say the least, but it was our story. My pretty girl had become everything to Me, and I would love her, honor her, and protect her and My family until My last days on earth.

Believe Me when I say that love doesn't appear when you want it to. It appears when you're ready for it, and in the most unusual manner.

Embrace it, accept it, and nurture it, even if it seems taboo. And it will bring you the sweetest things.

The End

Acknowledgments

Violette Dubrinksy: Thank you for creating a wonderful virtual world. Without Fantasyland to facilitate my inspiration, none of this would be happening!

Crystal Moody: You posted a photo during Scene Writing Sunday and a story was born. Thank you for the inspiration.

I also want to say thank you to my fabulous team of amazing people who all had a hand in making this novel happen: Laurel Cremant, Taria A. Reed, Crystal Rae, Daphne W., Alison Velea, Allyn Lesley, Heather Hope, Carolyn P., KJ, and lastly, my beta readers Tamara and Patrice.

LV, Vera, Phyllis, Margaret: Thank you for your support!

A special thank you to the bloggers and street teams who have been extremely helpful with spreading the word about this novel! I appreciate all that you do.

Thank you for your support! I would be most appreciative if you took a moment to leave a review on one of the following retail platforms: Amazon, Kobo, B&N, or iBooks. Reader feedback is imperative to an author's success. Positive and negative feedback is welcome.

STAY CONNECTED:

authorharpermiller@gmail.com

facebook.com/authorharpermiller

twitter.com/authorharpmill

goodreads.com/authorharpmill

plus.google.com/+HarperMillerAuthor

instagram.com/authorharpermiller

Sign up for exclusive content, ARC opportunities, and giveaways at my website:
www.authorharpermiller.com

ABOUT THE AUTHOR

Harper Miller is a thirty-something native New Yorker. She's traveled the world and lived in a variety of places but always finds her way back to the Big Apple. A lackluster love life leaves time to explore new interests; for Harper it is writing. *The Sweetest Taboo: An Unconventional Romance* is her debut novel. In her mind, the perfect Alpha male possesses intellect, humor, and a kinky streak that rivals the size of California.

When she isn't writing, Harper utilizes her graduate degree in the field of medical research. She enjoys fitness-related activities, drinking copious amounts of wine, and going on bad dates.

Printed in Great Britain
by Amazon